arrival

The PHOENIX FILES

Chris Morphew

arrival

Kane Miller
A DIVISION OF EDC PUBLISHING

First American Edition 2012
Kane Miller, A Division of EDC Publishing

Design by Sandra Nobes
Typesetting by Ektavo

First published in Australia in 2009 by Hardie Grant Egmont

For information contact:
Kane Miller, A Division of EDC Publishing
P.O. Box 470663
Tulsa, OK 74147-0663
www.kanemiller.com
www.edcpub.com

Library of Congress Control Number: 2011935699

Printed and bound in the United States of America
1 2 3 4 5 6 7 8 9 10
ISBN: 978-1-61067-091-3

To Melody,
Grace and Peace.
See you when I get home.

Chapter 1

The end of the world is one of those things that you never really expect to end up being *your* problem.

Not that I used to spend much time thinking about that kind of stuff. But if I had, I would've thought it was pretty safe to assume that saving the planet would be someone else's job.

So when we flew out to Phoenix a couple of weeks ago, it never really entered my head that I might be triggering a countdown to the destruction of the human race, or that I'd be the one who had to try to stop it.

We were supposed to be taking off from Sydney Airport at 2 p.m. But when the car from Mum's new company came to pick us up, our driver said there'd been a change of plans. He took us an hour out of the city to a private airstrip in the middle of a field. There was a helicopter waiting for us, this big ex-military thing. They'd ripped everything out of the back cabin and crammed in some airplane-style passenger seats. The windows had all been painted over, blocking our view of outside.

I thought the whole thing was more than a little weird, but Mum didn't have a problem with it, and I wasn't about to argue. She'd been accusing me for weeks of having a bad attitude about moving to Phoenix, and in her head, this would just prove her right. As if *my* attitude had caused all this in the first place.

It wasn't like I couldn't handle moving. Mum and Dad had always made sure I had plenty of practice. They both had high-powered jobs that meant we never stayed in one place for more than a year or two.

But this time I was leaving more behind than just a rental house and a school.

Two months back, the divorce papers had finally gone through. Dad had moved out a while before then, but now it was all official. Now they had the documentation to *prove* that the last seventeen years were just a sorry mistake.

Not exactly the greatest self-esteem boost for the son they'd had two years in.

They both tried to make it easy on me. They said all the stuff you're supposed to say to your kid when you split up.

Just because your father is moving out doesn't mean you won't get to see him.

Don't ever think that any of this is your fault.

We both still love you very much.

PS – I'm moving to some backwoods town a billion miles from nowhere and I'm taking you with me.

That last one wasn't quite so comforting.

Right after the divorce was finalized, Mum was approached by an organization called the Shackleton Co-operative who offered her this amazing job. I'm not sure why exactly, but for Mum it was like winning the lottery. There was just one little catch: she had to move out to Phoenix, this brand-new

3

corporate town built by the Shackleton Co-operative for all its employees. Which meant that I had to move, too.

Of course, Dad tried to keep her from taking me, but Mum had the better lawyers. Eventually, they worked out some deal where I'd live with her most of the time and fly back to see Dad for holidays and the odd weekend. My opinion never really came into it.

Anyway, that's how I wound up sitting in the back of a helicopter, flying out to a town so new and so tiny that no one had even been able to show it to me on a map.

I leaned my seat back as far as it would go and sat there listening to the thumping of the chopper blades above my head, eyes closed against the too-bright fluorescent lights that burned down from the ceiling. Mum sat in the seat next to mine, flicking through a copy of *Business Week*. She kept glancing down at me out of the corner of her eye, like she was trying to find something to say to reassure me, or at least stop me being so mad at her.

"I've heard wonderful things about your new school, Luke," she tried eventually.

"Yeah, you were saying."

"And you won't be the only new student, either. The whole town is still getting established, so there'll be plenty of others who haven't been around for long."

"Yeah."

She looked like she wanted to say something else, but then she bit her tongue and went back to her magazine.

And that was pretty much it for conversation.

The sky was just starting to grow darker as we got out of the helicopter at Phoenix Airport. Not that you could really call it an airport. It was basically just a clearing in the bush with a little landing strip and a house-sized gray building off to the side. There were a couple of other choppers and a sixteen-seater plane, and that was it.

Two men came up to us as we walked away from the chopper. One was dressed in jeans and a T-shirt. He was kind of overweight and had this massive Colonel Mustard moustache. The other guy was like a wall of solid muscle. He wore a black uniform with the same Shackleton Co-operative crest I'd seen on all the paperwork they'd been sending Mum – a red bird with its wings curved up into a circle.

"Welcome to Phoenix!" said Colonel Mustard, shaking our hands. "I'm Aaron Ketterley, Residential Liaison. I'll be showing you to your new place."

"Emily Hunter." Mum flashed her professional networking smile. "This is my son, Luke."

"Pleasure to meet you both," Mr. Ketterley beamed. He waved a hand at the stony-faced guy next to him. "Officer Bruce Calvin, Chief of Security."

The chief nodded at us, but didn't say anything.

"This way," said Mr. Ketterley, leading us across the tarmac to the terminal building.

Inside, it was like any other small-town airport – vending machines, a sea of blue seats, tired-looking staff behind marble counters – except that everything here was obviously brand new. There didn't seem to be any other passengers around, no one waiting for a flight. Just the airport staff and a security guy dressed in the same uniform as Officer Calvin.

As soon as we walked through the door, I pulled out my phone to call Dad.

No reception. Great.

"Hey, is there a phone somewhere?" I asked, avoiding Mum's eye. "I want to call my dad."

Mr. Ketterley frowned. "Sorry, buddy, all our phone lines are down at the moment. Internet, too. Our tech guys are working on it, though. We'll be back online before –"

"We should get you to your new place before it gets dark," Officer Calvin cut in, glancing sideways at him.

"Right," said Mr. Ketterley, clapping his hands together. He pulled two helmets down from a rack on the wall and tossed one to each of us.

"What's this for?" asked Mum, fumbling to catch her helmet.

"For the ride into town," said Mr. Ketterley. "Come on now, your bikes are around the back."

Mum stared at him. "Excuse me?"

"Ms. Hunter, car use is highly restricted in Phoenix. We're only a small town and we find that bikes are the most convenient way of getting around."

Now I was staring at him, too. I'm all for saving the environment, but come on, what kind of town doesn't let you drive a car?

"I haven't ridden a bike in years," Mum protested.

"Don't worry," smiled Mr. Ketterley, "it'll all come back to you. It's just like riding a ... well, you know. In any case, it's only a short ride."

"Define short."

"Oh, forty-five minutes or so."

Mum pursed her lips. It's what she always does when she's torn between demanding her own way and wanting to make a good impression.

"That sounds fine," she said, finally.

We found our bikes and rode away from the airport, down a wide dirt path that curved off into the bushland.

"Beautiful, huh?" said Ketterley, sweeping his arm out in front of him. "This bush stretches all the way around the town."

"What happens if it catches fire?" I asked.

Out of the corner of my eye, I caught a glimpse of Mum grinning. She reckons I worry too much. I thought it was a pretty fair question, though. If you're going to live out in the middle of nowhere, you want to know you're safe, right?

"No need to worry about that," said Mr. Ketterley.

"Phoenix's Security Center is equipped with the best firefighting gear on the planet. All of our safety and security systems are absolutely cutting edge."

And yet you can't even keep your phones up and running? I thought.

We kept riding, and eventually some buildings came into view up ahead. A few minutes later, we reached the edge of the town, and I realized just how seriously Phoenix took their No Cars policy. There wasn't a single real road in sight. Where the roads should have been, there was a sprawling network of bike tracks.

Mr. Ketterley took us down a wide track that led between two rows of houses. They were all identical – big, two-story, green-roofed buildings with low picket fences and perfectly mown lawns.

It was starting to get really dark now, and the streetlights were flickering on over our heads. We rode past a woman working in her garden. Mr. Ketterley waved at her as we went by. She smiled and waved back.

It was the perfect town. Almost too perfect. Like something out of *The Brady Bunch*.

"Ah," said Mr. Ketterley, coming to a stop. "Here we are, 43 Acacia Way. Welcome to your new home!" He pulled out a set of keys and handed them to Mum. "Someone will swing by in an hour or so to drop off your luggage."

"Great," said Mum, sounding breathless. "Thanks."

"Anything else I can help you with before I keep moving?"

"No," Mum said impatiently, then checked herself. "No, thank you."

"Right," said Mr. Ketterley brightly. "Well then, I'll leave you to it. Again, welcome to Phoenix! It's wonderful to have you as part of the family."

He shook our hands again and rode back towards the town center. We parked our bikes on the front porch and got ready to head inside.

"Luke," said Mum, stopping at the front door and putting her hand on my arm. "Listen. I know this isn't an ideal situation. Moving so suddenly like this, and so far away from your father. But it's not the end of the world. I think it'll be good for both of us. A clean break."

I thought of arguing. I thought of telling her that she was the only one who needed a clean break, and that I had been perfectly happy with my old life (minus all the arguing and screaming and divorcing, anyway). But I knew there'd be no point. I just nodded and let her pull me into a hug.

Not the end of the world.

Over the next few days, I was going to find out just how wrong she was.

Chapter 2

A blast of music rang out across the room and suddenly I was awake. I fumbled around for my phone and switched off the alarm. It took me a minute to remember where I was.

Huh? What happened to my –?

Oh. New house. Right.

I rolled out of bed and staggered into the hall, feeling vaguely uneasy. It's always weird waking up in a new house, and it didn't help that everything here was so abnormally *tidy*. I squinted around stupidly, reminding myself where the bathroom was.

"Morning, Luke," called Mum from below me. She

was halfway down the stairs, already up and dressed.

"Mmph," I said, my brain still kicking into gear.

"I'm on my way out the door. There's a bit of food in the kitchen, someone dropped off a welcome hamper about ten minutes ago. There's a town map on the counter – don't worry, it's very straightforward – and I've left you some money in case you want something else for lunch. I'll try to do a real shop tonight, but it might end up being takeout for dinner. Are you okay to get yourself to school?"

I nodded, yawning, my brain only registering about half of what she'd said.

"Okay, good. Have a great day, sweetheart. I'll see you tonight."

"Yeah, see you."

I stumbled into the bathroom, splashed some water on my face, and felt slightly more awake. Heading back to my room, I flipped my phone open again and squinted at the time.

8:07 a.m.

School started at nine, but I was supposed to get there early so that the principal could show me around. The usual first-day-of-school thing.

When I opened my closet, I found it already filled with school clothes – gray pants, white shirts, red ties. All in my size, too, which was weird. I didn't think Mum even knew what size I was anymore. There was a backpack as well, filled with books and pens and stuff.

I got dressed and went downstairs to find some breakfast.

Our new house was incredible. I'd always lived in nice houses, I guess, but this place was like something out of a home and garden magazine. High ceilings and paintings on the walls and giant indoor plants and light streaming in through enormous windows. Everything perfectly neat and tidy and expensive-looking.

The Shackleton Co-operative had insisted that we leave our old furniture behind and let them buy us all new stuff. Most people probably would've counted their blessings or whatever, but for some reason it put me kind of on edge. This place was meant to be my new home, and I felt like I wasn't supposed to touch anything. But I shook the feeling off and grabbed some fruit from the basket on the counter.

Ten minutes later, I was riding through the busy town center. I was still getting used to the whole bike-riding thing and I almost ran down about five people as I made my way through the morning traffic.

Everywhere I looked, there were men in black security uniforms, like the one Officer Calvin had been wearing the night before. Each of them had a gun holstered to his side. Maybe that's normal for security guards, but there was still something off-putting about them.

Halfway down the street, opposite the massive fountain in the town square, was a building covered in dark, tinted windows, those ones that make the whole thing look like a giant black mirror. The words *SHACKLETON CO-OPERATIVE* were emblazoned across the top of the building in big silver letters, next to a giant-sized version of the Phoenix logo on the guards' uniforms.

Back in Sydney, I wouldn't have looked twice at a building like that. But here in this tiny town where everything else was so clean and bright and friendly-looking, there was just something *wrong* about it. Like the people who put it there were trying to make a statement. *Don't forget who's in charge here.*

I kept glancing back over my shoulder at the building as I continued up to the school.

Phoenix High was at the end of the street, right across the road from Phoenix Mall. Creative naming was clearly not a high priority around here. There were kids in school uniforms milling around, getting breakfast from a burger place that looked like Phoenix's version of McDonald's.

It was hard to believe that a student had ever set foot in this school before today. There was no trash. No graffiti. Not one blade of grass out of place. And the buildings looked like they'd never been touched, like the cement was still drying between the bricks.

I chained my bike up at one of the hundreds of bike racks scattered all over the place and looked around for the front office.

The office lady smiled at me as I walked in the door. "Ah, you must be Luke Hunter," she said warmly. "Wait just a moment and I'll tell Mrs. Stapleton you're here."

"Oh," I said, surprised to be recognized so quickly. "Okay, thanks."

The office lady got up and walked out of the room. She came back almost immediately, followed by a serious-looking woman carrying a black bag.

"Luke," said the woman, extending a hand for me to shake. "Welcome. I'm Mrs. Stapleton, the deputy principal here at Phoenix High."

She smiled the smile shared by deputy principals all around the world, the one that says, *I'm being friendly now, but put a foot out of line and I'll destroy you.*

"Hi," I said. "Thanks."

"Our principal, Ms. Pryor, sends her apologies for not being here to greet you, but she's been held back at a meeting." Mrs. Stapleton held out the black bag. "Here, this is yours."

"What is it?" I asked.

"Your new laptop. Every student receives one when they arrive."

I took the bag and was suddenly reminded unpleasantly of my mum.

Right after my parents told me they were separating, which was about a month after I'd figured it out for myself, Mum went on this gift-giving spree. Almost every day, she'd come home with some new DVD or video game or whatever. It was like she thought that if she gave me enough stuff, I'd be too distracted to notice or care that my family was disintegrating around me.

And between the new bike, the new house, the massive TV in my room, and now this new laptop, it was almost enough to make me wonder if the people who ran this town were trying to pull the same distraction tactics.

Mrs. Stapleton walked outside and gestured for me to follow her. "As you may have heard, our external internet connection is down at the moment, but your computer will still be able to send and receive emails within Phoenix through our town intranet."

She stopped in the middle of the quad and looked around. A guy dashed past and she called out to him, "Peter, may I see you for a moment?"

He rolled his eyes and walked over to us. "It wasn't me, miss, it was Tank! He was trying to hit me with a trash can, and –"

"Peter, what class have you got for first period today?" asked Mrs. Stapleton, interrupting him.

"Um, English with Mr. Larson."

18

"Excellent," said Mrs. Stapleton. "Peter, this is Luke Hunter. He arrived yesterday. Will you show him around?"

"Sure, no worries, miss," Peter grinned.

"I'm trusting you to be sensible here, Peter," frowned Mrs. Stapleton.

"Of course, miss!"

Mrs. Stapleton shot Peter a suspicious glance, but didn't say anything more. She turned and went back into the office.

"Luke, right?" said Peter, moving off towards a building at the other end of the quad. "Let's go find your locker." He was a tall, weedy guy with messy brown hair, and he walked across the school like he owned the place. He seemed like a weird choice for the show-the-new-kid-around job.

"Don't you need to know my locker number?" I asked, following him.

"Nah," said Peter. "They're all in order of arrival. You'll be after Jordan."

"Huh?"

"Whenever someone new comes, they just give them the next locker in line," Peter explained as

19

he led me down a crowded corridor. "And *everyone* here is pretty new. I've only been in town for six months and I was one of the first to get here. That's why Staples gets me to show you guys around, even though she hates me, because I'm practically the only one who knows where everything is."

We stopped right at the end of the corridor.

"Huh," said Peter. "Look."

"What?" I asked.

"You've got the last locker."

"Does that mean something?" I asked, opening the locker door. I pulled a pen and a notebook out of my backpack and stashed the rest of my stuff inside.

"Dunno," said Peter. "I guess it means you're the last one coming."

Chapter 3

WEDNESDAY, MAY 6
99 DAYS

"What do you mean, the last one coming?" I said, my hand tensing up against the locker door as someone pushed past me. "You just said there are new people arriving all the time."

"Yeah," said Peter, "but I think this town is kind of invite-only. I mean, Shackleton built it for all the people who work at his company, right? And who else would want to live out here?"

"So, what, you're telling me this school knew in advance how many of us were going to be here and ordered that *exact* number of lockers?"

Peter shrugged. "So?"

Before I could reply, the bell rang and everyone started moving towards their classrooms.

"This way," said Peter, heading around a corner and up some more stairs. "Larson's an all right teacher. Hardly ever makes us do any actual work."

"Hey!" called a small voice from behind us as we made our way along another corridor. "Hey, uh, you – wait!"

A kid who looked like he was probably in Year 7 came running up to Peter. He was wearing a backpack that was almost as big as he was and he had a panicked look in his eyes.

"Excuse me," he said in a rush, "I have a history class in room nine and I can't remember –"

"Back down the stairs," said Peter wearily. "Hang a right, then go down to the end of the hall."

"Thank you!" squeaked the kid, running off again.

"Honestly," said Peter, shaking his head, "I should be getting paid for this."

By the time we got to the English room, a bunch of other students were already waiting.

"Hey, Weir!" shouted a girl at the back as soon as we walked in. "Who's that?"

This girl was pretty and she knew it. She had wavy blonde hair and *Days of our Lives* makeup, and was sitting on a desk in front of two boys.

"This is Luke," Peter called back. "Got here yesterday, I think." He was acting casual enough, but the way his eyes flashed between the three of them as we walked over made me wonder if there was something going on. He turned to me and pointed to each of them in turn. "Cathryn, Tank, Michael."

It wasn't hard to see where Tank got his nickname. He was tall and wide, and clearly not the sharpest tool in the shed. He looked like he could easily roll right over the top of me. Michael, meanwhile, was hunched over a piece of paper, working on an elaborate drawing of two men in flowing white robes. He wore dark sunglasses and black nail polish and he was clutching his pencil like that drawing was the most important thing in the world to him.

Michael seemed like the sort of guy who probably would've gotten beat up a lot at my last school. But

I doubted anyone was going to mess with him while Tank was around.

For a minute, Peter looked like he was going to sit down next to them, but then he turned away and started moving across to the other side of the room.

"Friends of yours?" I asked, as we shuffled our way between two rows of desks.

"Used to be, yeah," he said under his breath.

There was a definite edge to Peter's voice now, but I figured I should wait until I'd known him longer than ten minutes before I started hammering him with personal questions.

We found two empty chairs and sat down. In the row behind us, a girl who looked like she might be Fijian or something was reading over a page of math questions. She had black hair all done up in little braids and a look of frustration on her face. She was pretty, but not in a self-conscious way like Cathryn.

"Hey, Jordan," said Peter, turning around to talk to her.

"Something I can do for you, Weir?"

"Just wanted to say that you're no longer Phoenix

High's newest inmate," said Peter, waving a hand in my direction.

"Wonderful," said Jordan, not looking up from her paper.

Peter gave me a weary look. "She's kind of in love with me," he whispered. "It's a bit embarrassing, actually."

I raised an eyebrow at him.

"No, seriously! She may try to hide her feelings behind that harsh exterior, but deep down I know she's – *ow!*"

I turned around. Jordan had just nailed Peter in the back of the head with an eraser.

"See?" he said, bending down to pick it up. "Text-book love-hate relationship."

Jordan just rolled her eyes.

"This is going to bruise," said Peter, sitting up and rubbing his head. "Seriously, there's a lump here. I should report you to Staples, Jordan. Violence against a fellow student, that's not something we take lightly around here."

Jordan held up a hand like she was about to

slap him. "Keep whingeing, Weir, and I'll give you something to really cry about."

She was kidding, I think.

Peter grinned at her and opened his mouth to say something else, but at that moment Mr. Larson walked into the room. He was wearing a shirt and tie and carrying a big plastic crate. He looked young for a teacher, but not someone you could just walk all over.

"Morning, everyone," he said, putting the crate down on his desk.

"Hey, sir!" said Peter, sticking a hand into the air. "We've got another newbie."

"Oh yes, they told me about you," said Mr. Larson. "Luke Hunter, right?"

"Yeah," I said, bracing for the tell-us-a-bit-about-yourself speech.

But Mr. Larson just went straight on with the lesson. "You have impeccable timing, Luke," he said, reaching into his crate, "because today we are starting a brand-new book study."

Everyone else groaned as Mr. Larson started handing out fresh copies of some novel – *The Shape of Things to Come.*

"I'd like you all to read this in the next two weeks," said Mr. Larson.

"What?" shouted Tank from the back. "Come on, sir! Be reasonable!"

"However," Mr. Larson smiled, "I realize that this is about as likely as Peter ever getting that haircut he so desperately needs." He pushed a button on his desk and a projector screen came down from the ceiling. "So today we're going to begin by watching the movie adaptation."

The class cheered.

"Let me warn you," Mr. Larson continued, walking over to turn off the lights, "that this is only a starting point. You *will* need to read the book at some stage, and rest assured I will know if you haven't done so."

The movie turned out to be pretty dodgy. It was this ancient black and white thing from the 1930s with lame special effects, but even a bad movie is better than doing a worksheet or whatever.

A couple of boys wandered in about halfway through the lesson, muttering something about a mixed-up timetable. Mr. Larson just handed each of them a copy of the book and pointed to some empty chairs at the back of the room.

That was a good sign. Obviously this guy had a bit of perspective.

But as the day went on, I realized that people showing up late or wandering into the wrong room were fairly regular features of life at Phoenix High. Like Mum had predicted, I was a long way from being the only new kid in this place. Even some of the teachers didn't seem totally on top of things.

Apart from that, though, Phoenix High wasn't that different from the last three high schools I'd been at. The only other major difference was that, like the rest of the town, this place was obviously running on a gazillion-dollar budget, so everything in it was top-of-the-line.

I ended up sticking with Peter for most of the day. After whatever had happened between him and his old friends, I got the feeling he was grateful to have someone new to hang out with. When the final bell went, the two of us grabbed our identical bikes and walked them back out onto the main street.

"What's up with all the security guards?" I asked as we passed another guy in a black uniform.

"They work for Mr. Shackleton," said Peter. "We have them here instead of cops."

"Instead of cops? Is that even legal?"

"Must be."

"But doesn't the government make sure there's police everywhere?" I asked. "Isn't that a rule?"

"I dunno," said Peter. "But it's not as if we need both. Phoenix has, like, zero crime."

A bit further up the road, Peter stopped at the big fountain in the town square. "This is my stop," he said, thrusting a thumb over his shoulder at the tall, black building I'd noticed on my way in. "My dad's finishing work early today and I'm supposed to meet him here."

I stared up at the building. "What is that place anyway?"

"Shackleton Building," said Peter. "Just offices and meeting rooms and stuff. Like our town hall, I guess."

"Pretty big town hall," I muttered. I knew I was

probably starting to sound paranoid, but I couldn't shake the feeling there was more to the building than that. "Is that all that goes on in there? Just meetings?"

"Uh-huh," Peter said blankly. "Well, just that and the alien autopsies."

I rolled my eyes and his face broke into a grin.

"Mate, just because a building's big and black and shiny doesn't mean there's something suss going on inside."

"All right, all right," I said, slightly frustrated, but trying not to show it. "Sorry."

"It's all good," said Peter. "But just try to relax, will you? I know Phoenix can seem a bit weird at first, but it's an okay town once you get used to it."

"Yeah. Well, see you tomorrow, okay?"

"Yeah, see you."

I flipped my mobile open for about the hundredth time that day. Still no reception.

How long would it take Dad to start worrying that he hadn't heard from us?

I hopped on my bike and rode the rest of the way home, my frustration building. As soon as I got inside, I went into the kitchen and tried the land line. No dial tone. The lines were still down.

Unbelievable. How much longer did they think this place could keep functioning without phones?

Get a grip, I told myself. *They're working on it.*

Maybe Peter was right. Maybe I was just stressing out over nothing. This place wasn't all bad. As far as first days at a new school went, this one had been pretty good.

By the time I got to the top of the stairs, I was almost ready to take his advice and forget about the few little things that had been bugging me about Phoenix.

But then I opened my bedroom door.

Have you ever had one of those moments where all of a sudden you just *know* that something really, really bad is coming? One of those moments where, somehow, even though there's no real sign of anything being wrong, you just feel it in your gut that there's major trouble on the way?

As I walked into my bedroom and glanced at my bed, I was punched in the face by one of those moments.

Someone had been in here.

Someone had come into my room and made my bed.

Sitting on top of the pillow was a small, unmarked yellow envelope.

And before I opened it up, before I even touched that envelope, I *knew* there was nothing but trouble inside.

Chapter 4

Hang on, I told myself, glancing around the room. *Calm down. Maybe this is normal. Maybe we have a cleaning service.*

But no, nothing else in the room had been touched. My pajamas were lying on the floor in the corner. A half-empty glass of water was still sitting on my bedside table.

Whoever had been in here hadn't been invited.

I gritted my teeth and grabbed a textbook from my desk to defend myself. Because clearly their guns and meat cleavers would be no match for my *Studies in Geography.*

I walked back out into the hall and started checking through the whole house room by room, trying not to think too much about what might happen if there actually *was* someone else in here.

But the whole house was deserted. Nothing missing. Nothing even moved. And I couldn't see any sign of someone forcing their way in.

Except for the envelope sitting on my bed.

I went back into my room and picked it up, turning it over in my hands. No name, no address. There was something small and solid sliding around inside. I tore open the envelope and tipped the thing into my hand.

It was a USB memory stick. Expensive-looking. Silver stainless steel. There were two letters on the side that looked like they'd been scratched into the metal with a paperclip: *J.B.*

Someone's initials, maybe? The original owner's?

But why would they go to all the trouble of breaking into my house and delivering me a secret message or whatever, if the initials on the stick were just going to lead me straight back to them?

I pulled out my new laptop and drummed my

fingers on the desk as it started up. My mind was flashing back to every movie I'd ever seen about an apparently normal kid being contacted by a secret spy agency or told they had hidden superpowers.

Don't be an idiot. It's probably just…

But I had no idea what it probably was.

The computer finally finished loading and I plugged in the USB. A folder popped up on the screen, showing the contents of the stick. There was only one file on it:

intSC1002A_lhunter.doc

L. Hunter. So this was definitely meant for me.

I opened up the file. It was a huge stream of garbled text, pages and pages of it, like someone had let their two-year-old loose on the computer and sent me the results.

I tried opening the file up in another program. Nothing.

Maybe this was all just a prank. Some stupid mind game that the kids at school played with new arrivals. But how could they have gotten inside the house?

Then I remembered something: the principal, Ms. Pryor, hadn't been around today. Could she have had something to do with this?

Yes, Luke, your new school principal (who you've never even met) took the day off school to sneak into your house and drop off a memory stick filled with gibberish.

And make your bed.

Right. That made sense.

I closed my eyes and dropped back into my chair. This was going nowhere.

But then I thought back to our computer studies lesson from that afternoon. We'd been given the whole period to turn some climate change data into a graph, but Peter had finished in about four seconds. Maybe he'd have more luck with this.

Obviously a phone call wasn't an option, but Mrs. Stapleton had said that the town's intranet was still working. I found Peter's address in the town directory and emailed him about the USB, trying to sound as casual as possible, not wanting to give him another excuse to accuse me of worrying over nothing. I attached the garbled file and hit send.

While I was at it, I tried sending an email through to Dad. It bounced straight back.

I spun around in my chair and my eyes landed

back on my neatly-made bed. Somehow, those perfectly tucked-in sheets added a whole other layer of creepiness. I mean, why bother? Surely being a mysterious stalker was weird enough without being a neat freak as well.

I glanced over my shoulder, trying to shake the feeling of unseen eyes bearing down on me, and went back to my school bag. Already, I had a ton of homework to do. Four pages of trigonometry questions and a research assignment on cyclones.

I tried to make a start on it all, but with everything else buzzing around in my head, it was impossible to concentrate and I wound up lying on my bed watching TV instead.

There was nothing on. As in, literally nothing. Every channel I flipped to was just a white screen with a Shackleton Co-operative logo that said, *150 Satellite Channels COMING SOON!*

I finally came across the one channel that *was* working, but it was just this lame "Welcome to Phoenix" movie playing on a loop. The camera followed a way-too-perfect-looking man and woman around the town as they smiled and waved and gushed about how amazing and wonderful and environmentally-friendly everything was.

I watched the rest of the video, then waited for the next loop and watched the whole thing through again. Apart from the overly enthusiastic hosts (seriously, no one is *that* excited about water filtration), there was no sign of anything weird going on in the town.

Of course not. The whole point of this movie was to show that Phoenix was normal. Better than normal.

There was a game console sitting on top of the TV cabinet. I thought again about doing some homework, but decided to go easy on myself. First day of school and all that. So I sat on my bed playing video games until about 7:30 p.m., when Mum finally got home.

"Luke! Dinner!"

I went downstairs and found her walking into the family room with a stack of papers in one hand and a pizza box in the other.

"Sorry I'm so late," she said, putting them down on the coffee table and collapsing onto a couch. "Wall-to-wall orientation meetings all day. It was

38

four-thirty before they even showed me to my office."

Mum's a human resources manager. Basically, her work involves getting paid through the nose by some huge company or other to figure out how they can get the most out of their employees for the least amount of money.

"No worries," I said, barely hearing her. Mum's been apologizing for staying late at work for as long as I can remember.

"I'll shop tomorrow," Mum yawned. "At least enough to cook you a real dinner."

"Right," I said, knowing she wouldn't. Dad had always been in charge of the cooking at home, and there'd been a pretty disgusting drop in the amount of real food we ate since he moved out.

"How was school?"

"All right," I said, grabbing a slice of pizza and sitting down on one of the other couches, still feeling like a stranger in my own house. My mind flashed to the USB sitting upstairs on my desk, but I didn't really see any point in telling Mum about it. "The phones are still down," I added.

Mum nodded. "It's the same all over town. I

spoke to my boss about it. Apparently they've been off-line for almost a month now."

"Huh?" I looked up from my pizza. "Seriously? What's taking so long?"

"She didn't say," Mum said with a shrug. "But Phoenix is a small town, and fairly isolated. And don't forget, this whole place was built from the ground up less than a year ago. There were bound to be a few hiccups along the way."

"A month with no phones? You call that a hiccup?"

"What do you want me to call it? Obviously it's not ideal, but they'll sort it all out soon enough. And in the meantime, the intranet is still up and running. So, really, it's not such a huge problem."

Of course not. Unless your father is hundreds of kilometers away and completely unreachable.

I didn't say it out loud, but I must have made a face because Mum shot me a concerned look and said, "What's wrong?"

"Nothing," I muttered, not at all interested in getting into another conversation about her and Dad.

I went straight back upstairs after dinner, made

a vague attempt at getting on with my homework again, and then decided to go to bed instead.

I was just on the brink of sleep when I heard something beeping from across the room. I staggered over to my laptop, still sitting open on the desk. A white envelope was blinking in the corner of the screen. A reply to my email.

I clicked on the envelope and the message popped up on my screen.

> *sorry mate no idea what this is – the file looks like it's been*
> *corrupted*
> *the only J.B. I can think of is Jordan from school… maybe*
> *check her out tomorrow?*
> *bring the USB too so I can have a look at it*
> *Peter*

I closed the laptop and went back to bed, telling myself I was just overreacting. Whatever this was about, there was no way it could be as serious as I was imagining.

Chapter 5

I woke up way too early the next morning, with the sudden urge to get out of our creepy display home of a house. I yelled goodbye to Mum through the bathroom door and rode out into the main street to get some breakfast.

The sun was still coming up, but there were already plenty of people around. They were mostly security guards or business types. But as I rode past the fountain, I saw a guy who was definitely not on his way to the office.

His hair, beard, and clothes were all brown and ratty. His arms and his face were completely covered with gashes and scars, like he'd been caught in a fire or something years ago. He was probably about thirty, but he was so disfigured that it was hard to tell. It might have been my imagination, but I was sure I could smell him from across the fountain. As I watched, he reached into a trash can and pulled out a half-finished cup of coffee.

A homeless guy, *here?* It didn't seem right. I mean, not that it's ever right for people to be homeless, but in picture-perfect Phoenix this guy stuck out like a sore thumb.

The man stared at me as I rode past, his eyes following me down the street. I wondered whether I should turn back and give him money or something, but in the end I just kept on riding. Looking over my shoulder, I saw him chug down the coffee and drop the cup back into the trash.

"That's just Crazy Bill," said Peter, when he arrived at school a couple of hours later. "He's our resident hobo."

"That's what people call him? Crazy Bill?"

43

"Yeah, I guess Psychologically-Disturbed-But-Probably-Still-Pretty-Nice Bill doesn't have quite the same ring to it," said Peter. He was sitting hunched over his laptop, rushing to finish a history essay that was apparently a week late.

"I thought you said this town was invite-only," I said. "Where did he come from?"

Peter shrugged. "Must've snuck in somehow. They usually try to keep him off the main street, but he's not really hurting anyone, is he?"

"Why doesn't somebody help him?"

"Dunno," said Peter, like the thought had never occurred to him. "I guess someone should, hey?" He typed a few more lines then looked up and said, "Stalin was World War II, right?"

"I think so."

"Awesome." He clicked print and closed his laptop. "So, show me this memory stick."

I reached into my pocket and pulled out the silver stick. Peter grabbed it and turned it over in his fingers, like a jeweler examining a diamond.

"I checked the town directory," he said, handing the USB back. "The only J.B.s are Jordan Burke and

Julian Burrows."

"Who's Julian Burrows?"

"Big fat maintenance guy who takes care of the fountains. I'm gonna assume he's not the one we're after." Peter stood up and we headed inside towards the print room.

"Okay, Jordan then. But why would she be sending me this?" I asked.

"Who knows?" said Peter. "Maybe she wants a date."

"What? I only got here two days ago! She hasn't even –" I shut up when I saw Peter laughing.

"Relax, mate, I'm only kidding. Anyway," he winked, "you wouldn't have a chance."

"Right," I said, smirking, "because clearly she's all over you."

"All in good time," Peter grinned, heading into the print room. He picked up his essay from the printer just as the bell went. "Come on. Assembly."

We walked back outside and followed the crowd down to the school hall. At most of my old schools, we used to have our assemblies sitting on plastic chairs in the gym. The Phoenix High hall was more like a theatre. There was a stage at the bottom with hundreds of cushy red seats in a semicircle around it.

"Who paid for all this?" I asked as we took two seats in the back row.

"Shackleton," said Peter distractedly. "Apparently, the Co-operative people are all mega-multi-billionaires. Probably built this place with the money they found under their couch cushions." He craned his neck, scanning the hall. "Where is she...?"

"So, what do you reckon this file is?" I lowered my voice to an undertone as some Year 7 kids sat down in the seats next to ours. "I mean, it's got to be *something*, right? Like a coded message or –"

"There," said Peter suddenly.

I looked in the direction he was pointing and saw Jordan sitting over on the other side of the hall. She was staring right at us. As soon as I caught her eye, she turned away. But she'd definitely been watching.

"We'll catch her on the way out," said Peter. "Figure out what's going on."

A voice from the stage cut our conversation short. "All right, ladies and gentlemen, let's make a start."

It was Mrs. Stapleton. The chatter around the hall quickly died down.

"Crap," hissed Peter. "I just lost five bucks."

"Huh?"

"Mike's taking bets on when Pryor will finally show up to run an assembly," Peter whispered, pointing down at the principal's empty seat on the stage. "I had five dollars that said it was gonna be today."

"She wasn't around when I got here yesterday," I said. "Mrs. Stapleton said she was in a meeting."

"Yeah," said Peter. "We've barely seen her since the start of the year. She's always holed up in her office."

"Doing what?"

"How should I know?" said Peter. "Principal stuff."

A teacher with thinning red hair was prowling the aisles, looking for troublemakers. He glared at us as he passed and we stopped talking.

All the cushy seating in the world couldn't save the assembly from being as mind-numbing as any other. After forty-five minutes of announcements, sports reports and a musical performance from the school string ensemble, we were finally let out, just as the bell went for our next class.

Right away, we started weaving our way towards Jordan. She looked up and saw us coming. For a minute, it looked like she wanted to stop and say something. But then she grabbed her bag and took off in the other direction.

"Try again at recess?" I suggested.

"No need," said Peter. "She's got design and tech next period. If we're quick, we can catch her before she gets there."

"You've memorized her timetable?" I said as we moved out into the quad.

"Can't blame a guy for doing his research," said Peter. "Look, there she is!"

Jordan looked back, spotted us, and started walking faster. She veered across towards the Industrial Arts building. We followed after her, almost running.

"Are you lost, Peter?"

Peter wheeled around. It was the balding teacher from assembly, looking murderous.

"No, Mr. Hanger," said Peter, smiling innocently. "We were just —"

"Excellent," said Mr. Hanger. "Then I'm sure you can find a more direct route to our history classroom.

Getting there on time today might be a nice change of pace, don't you think?"

"Yes, sir," said Peter, rolling his eyes.

The teacher turned back towards his room and we followed behind him. Glancing over my shoulder, I saw Jordan disappear into the IA building.

"Bloody Mr. Hanger," Peter muttered under his breath a few minutes later as we took our seats in the classroom. He pulled his crumpled history essay out of his bag and put it on the table in front of him.

I figured out pretty quickly why Peter hated Mr. Hanger so much. Nearly everyone did. He's one of those bitter old teachers who's angry with the whole world and spends most of his time taking it out on his students. He seemed really out of place at Phoenix High. All the other teachers I'd met so far had been clones of Mr. Larson – young and enthusiastic and excited about nurturing growing minds or whatever.

Mr. Hanger, on the other hand, passed out four worksheets he'd photocopied from a textbook and told us we weren't going anywhere until we'd finished them. As we worked, he sat at his desk reading a magazine and giving out detentions for stuff like coughing too much or asking to borrow a ruler.

By the time we finally escaped the class, recess was already half-over and the building was almost deserted. We headed for the lockers, figuring we could ambush Jordan when she came to get her stuff for next period.

"So what do we do when we see her?" I asked on our way down the stairs.

"What do you mean?"

"How do we get her to talk to us? I mean, she's obviously avoiding us. And we can't, like, *grab* her or anything..." I rounded the corner and froze.

Jordan was storming down the corridor towards us, fists clenching at her sides, cold fury on her face. She looked ready to beat the crap out of us. Peter opened his mouth to say something, but Jordan brushed straight past, ignoring him completely, closing in on me instead. She didn't stop until we were almost nose to nose.

"What do you want?" she demanded.

"Huh?" I said stupidly. I didn't really know how I'd expected the meeting to play out, but this definitely wasn't it. "Hang on –"

"You think I haven't seen you following me around all morning?" she shouted. "You think I don't know what *else* you've been up to?"

"Jordan, I don't –"

"You wanted to get my attention? Well, here I am. So, let's hear it!"

"Whoa, Jordan," said Peter, taking a step towards us. "Why are you getting so fired up?"

He put a hand on Jordan's shoulder and for a second I thought she was going to punch him. Instead, she took a couple of steps back from me, jabbed an arm in Peter's direction and said, "Tell him."

"I – what?" I said.

"Hunter, right?" said Jordan. "Luke Hunter?"

"Yeah, but –"

"Well, Luke, why don't *you* tell Weir what's gotten me so fired up?"

"Jordan," I said, bracing myself in case she attacked me or something, "I don't know what you're –"

"Tell him what you were doing yesterday after school!"

"He wasn't doing anything!" said Peter, clearly as lost as I was. "He was in town with me for like fifteen

51

minutes, then he went back to his place."

"Yeah?" said Jordan, whirling around to face me again. "Then who broke into my house and left *this?*"

She pulled something small and shiny from her skirt pocket. It was a USB, identical to the one I'd found in my room, except this one was engraved with a different set of initials. *L.H.*

"Look familiar?" she sneered, holding the thing up a centimeter from my face.

"Actually," I said, reaching down into my own pocket, careful not to make any sudden movements, "yeah, it kind of does."

I pulled out my own memory stick and held it up next to Jordan's.

Her eyes fell on the *J.B.* engraved on the side and the expression on her face changed completely. *"What?"*

"How about that?" said Peter, stepping forward and putting an arm around each of our shoulders. "I reckon the three of us have got some talking to do."

Chapter 6

THURSDAY, MAY 7
98 DAYS

"Sorry," said Jordan for about the hundredth time. "I'm really sorry. I just – it's this place. Ever since we moved here, I can't shake the feeling that there's something not *right* going on."

"Yeah, don't worry about it," I said. Not that I appreciated almost having my head bitten off, but I was glad to not be the only one who thought something was off about Phoenix.

It was lunchtime and the three of us were sitting in the back corner of the library, crowded around Peter's laptop. Math had been all pen-and-paper, so this was the first chance we'd had to figure out the memory sticks. Peter plugged Jordan's stick into his computer, bringing up a single text file.

intSC1002B_jburke.doc

He opened it up. Gibberish, just like mine.

"See?" said Jordan. "Nothing."

"I don't think it's nothing," said Peter. He brought up the file from my stick and put the two streams of text side by side.

"What is it, then?" I asked.

"I don't know," said Peter slowly, squinting at the screen as though he was seeing something that we couldn't. "But it's not nothing. It's definitely something."

"Oh, good," said Jordan. "Thanks for clearing that up." She leaned behind Peter to look at me. "Have you told your parents about this?"

"Nope," I said. "Dad's back in Sydney, so obviously I can't tell him. You know, with the phones and everything. And my mum's not exactly –"

"How come your dad's not here?" Peter cut in, turning to look at me.

"My parents aren't together anymore," I said, wondering why this needed spelling out.

Peter shot me a weird look. "Oh."

"That a problem?"

"No," he said quickly. "It's just a bit … surprising, that's all. The other families around here are all – I think you might be the only one whose parents aren't together."

"Nice going, Weir," said Jordan. "Way to make him feel included."

"I didn't mean –" Peter started.

"Forget it," I said.

Peter turned his attention back to the computer.

"What about you?" I asked Jordan. "Did you tell your parents?"

"No. I was going to. But they've got enough to worry about, so I thought I'd wait and –"

"Take me on yourself?" I suggested dryly.

"Well, yeah," she said, looking embarrassed.

"I guess that's the point of all this, though, isn't it?" I said. "I mean, someone's obviously gone to a lot of trouble to bring us together."

"What?" said Peter, his head snapping up. "You two?"

"Right," said Jordan. "The initials. They wanted us to find each other."

"And look at the file names," I said, pointing to the screen. "They're labeled A and B, see?"

intSC1002A_lhunter.doc

intSC1002B_jburke.doc

"What if they're two halves of the same message or code or whatever?" I added. "Like, what if we both only got part of the picture so we'd have to put them together?"

"Yeah," said Peter, making a face at the screen in front of him. He went to the top of my file and started adding what looked like more random letters to the first line.

"What are you doing?" I asked.

"Hang on," said Peter absently, fingers flashing across the keyboard.

"What I don't get, though, is why *us?*" Jordan said to me. "Even if that's all true, why did this person choose us two for … whatever this is? What do we even have in common?"

"You mean besides an irrational paranoia that this whole town is out to get you?" Peter muttered, still typing.

"Come on," I told him, "you still don't think

there's anything weird about all of this?"

"Of course it's weird," said Peter. "But you don't even know what this thing *says* yet. Might be worth waiting until we get that much figured out before you start going nuts with the conspiracy theories, don't you reckon?" He kept typing, his eyes flicking back and forth between the two streams of text.

"Peter," I said, "what are you –?"

"It's not a text file," said Peter.

"Huh?"

"You're right, it's one file split in half, but it's not a document. It's something else. A picture or a sound clip or – I don't know. Something." He stopped typing.

"Can you open it?" asked Jordan.

"I think so," Peter said, scrolling through the pages and pages of text, "but it'll take a while to put it all back together. I'll take the files home and work on it tonight."

"Don't you have to rewrite that essay for Mr. Hanger?" I asked.

"Stuff Mr. Hanger," said Peter with a wave of his hand. "Besides, how could I possibly concentrate on

57

homework with all this excitement going on?"

Jordan rolled her eyes at him. "You're an idiot. You know that, right?"

The bell rang and we went downstairs to our science classroom. Like everything else at Phoenix High, the lab was brand new and unnaturally clean.

Most of the class was already inside by the time we got there. The kids who weren't chucking paper balls around or harassing the fish in the tank next to the window were sitting in groups of two or three at white lab benches. The bench tops gleamed so brightly it was almost painful.

"Oi, Weir!" called a voice from across the room. "Pay up!"

I looked over and saw Michael sitting at a bench near the back, waving Peter over. Tank and Cathryn were with him.

Peter sighed and reached into his pocket. He pulled out a handful of coins, counted out five dollars, and dumped the money on the desk in front of Michael.

"Should've listened to me," said Michael pityingly, gathering up the coins and recounting them. "Way too early, man. Seriously, you should've paid me in advance and saved yourself the trouble."

Peter pulled up a stool at the bench behind them. "Hey, what can I say? I'm an optimist."

"Bah," said Michael, pocketing Peter's money. "Optimism is for the poor! Trust me, mate, it'll be at least another week before Pryor shows her face around here."

Jordan and I took the two empty spaces at Peter's bench. Cathryn swiveled around on her stool, sizing us both up.

"You hanging out with these two now?" she asked Peter, not taking her eyes off us.

Peter shrugged. "You want to give me a reason not to?"

I gave him a questioning look, but he was too fixated on Cathryn to notice.

"Do whatever you want," she said. "I just thought the last six months might have counted for a bit more than that."

"Hey, don't go making this about me!" Peter snapped. "Anytime one of you feels like letting me in on what you're all –"

"Pete, look," said Michael, turning around, "you know it's not up to us."

Peter got up off his stool, but before he had time to say anything else, a kid who'd been standing guard at the door pulled his head back into the room and yelled, "Benson's coming!"

Everyone raced to their seats and scrambled to pull out their laptops. Seconds later, a tall, skinny woman with red-framed glasses walked into the room. She glared at the class like she was sure we'd all been up to something, then turned around and wrote a heading up on the board.

Comparative Embryology

We all opened our laptops and copied down the heading in silence.

I glanced sideways at Peter, who was still staring daggers at the back of Michael's head. What in the world was all that about? The whole thing reminded me of what Mum and Dad were like near the end, when conversations could go from civil to screaming in twenty-five words or less.

Jordan turned to speak to Peter, probably looking for an explanation too, but he shot her a don't-want-to-talk-about-it look and she let it drop.

We spent the rest of the class making slide shows to explain how, when you get right down to it, every animal starts out as the same little orange blob. Or something.

This gave Peter a bit of time to work on recombining the files on his computer, quickly flashing up his science work whenever Ms. Benson walked past. By the time the lesson was over, he was still less than halfway done, but at least he'd calmed down a bit after his run-in with Cathryn.

And even though Peter thought the whole coded message thing was bit of a joke, Jordan managed to convince him to take the files straight home after school and keep working on them. Then again, I reckon Jordan could probably have convinced Peter to chop out his own tongue with a butter knife if she'd wanted to.

As soon as I got home, I made another pointless attempt at trying to get in touch with Dad, and then went upstairs, set my laptop up on my desk, and waited.

I tried to get through some of my growing pile

of homework, but I was too distracted. Peter had promised to let us know as soon as he figured anything out, and I kept stopping every two minutes to check if he'd emailed yet.

Mum came home at 7:00 p.m. with a takeout salad and two boxes of microwave macaroni and cheese. The closest thing she could manage to her promised home-cooked meal. I ate quickly and then raced back upstairs.

At 10:30 p.m., the reply from Peter finally came.

hey Luke

I figured out the message. turns out it's an audio file.

I've listened to it a couple of times already ... it's gotta be a joke, but I reckon you guys should probably hear it for yourselves.

meet me at the fountain tomorrow morning – 6:30 before it gets too crowded.

mate if this thing is legit ... we are all in some SERIOUS trouble.

Chapter 7

FRIDAY, MAY 8
97 DAYS

"About time," said Jordan as I pulled up next to the fountain in the morning and ditched my bike on the ground. She and Peter were already sitting on one of the wooden benches that surrounded the fountain, clutching coffee cups. "What took you so long?"

"What do you mean?" I yawned, grabbing my phone to check the time. I glanced at Peter, who for some reason was looking extremely pleased with himself. "You said six-thirty, right?"

"Huh?" said Jordan. "You told me six."

"Did I?" said Peter, quickly wiping the grin off his face. "Oh. Sorry."

Jordan turned her attention back to the computer sitting open on Peter's lap.

I shot a confused look at Peter, who winked at me behind Jordan's back. He performed a silent fake yawn and mimed putting an arm around her shoulder.

"Are you kidding?" I said. "Do you have to pull that crap right *now?*"

"Pull what crap?" said Jordan, looking up again.

"Nothing, don't worry," I muttered, sitting down next to Peter. "Have you listened to it yet?"

"No, we were waiting for you," said Jordan. She turned to Peter. "Go on. Show us."

"Wait a sec," I said, glancing up and down the street, checking to make sure we wouldn't be overheard.

As usual, there were a dozen or more security guards patrolling the street. Across the fountain, two of them were having an argument with Crazy Bill, who they'd just found sleeping under a tattered blanket in one of the gardens that decorated the town center. Then there was the normal crowd of business people riding by on bikes or lining up for coffee, but none of them seemed –

"Come on," said Peter impatiently. "Settle down,

will you? As if anyone walking past is going to care what three random teenagers are looking at on their computer."

"Fine," I said, turning back to the screen. "Go ahead, play it."

The clip was all muffled and distorted, like it had been recorded on a phone in someone's pocket. There was a tapping sound, footsteps maybe, then a warbled voice.

"I take it our final arrivals have landed?" the voice said. It was a man. He sounded like he might have been around my dad's age.

"Yes, sir," said a second, deeper-voiced man. "Aaron is showing them to their living quarters as we speak."

"Nothing concerning to report?" the first man asked easily.

There was the sound of a chair being pulled out. Then the second man spoke again. His voice sounded familiar, but it was hard to place through all the static.

"No, sir. The boy has a father on the outside with whom he was quite fixated on getting in touch, but –"

"That's me!" I said, suddenly realizing. "I asked to call my dad as soon as –"

"Shh!" hissed Jordan. I shut up and went back to the recording.

"I assume you explained the situation to him," the first man was saying.

"Yes, sir," said the second man. "Aaron made it clear that communication with the outside world is impossible."

"Good," said the first man. "I trust that Tabitha is prepared?"

"Yes, sir. Dr. Galton made the final adjustments this morning. We're ready to begin, pending your authorization."

"Excellent. Yes, by all means, begin the countdown."

"Yes, sir."

I glanced at Peter and Jordan, but from the looks on their faces they obviously couldn't make any more sense of this than I could.

There was a long pause. When the deep-voiced man spoke again, he sounded as though he was choosing his words very carefully.

"Sir," he said slowly, "might it not be wise to

66

commence final lockdown procedures ahead of schedule, now that all of our candidates are inside?"

"Bruce, we've been over this before," said the other man wearily. "The town has already been secured. You've made sure of that yourself. Any further action at this point would only create panic."

"My men would be more than capable of subduing –"

"At what cost, Bruce? We have two thousand candidates. That's all. We can't afford a blood bath."

"But, sir, if someone from the outside –"

"In a hundred days there won't *be* anyone left on the outside! Until that time, it is imperative that the people of Phoenix remain under the belief that their lives are progressing as normal."

There was another long silence. It took me a second to realize that I wasn't breathing.

"Yes, sir," said the deep-voiced man, eventually. "Of course."

"We're on the home stretch now, Bruce," the other man said. "When the countdown expires, Tabitha will cleanse the outside world of the human plague, and we who are left can get on with the business of rebuilding things. Until then, you and your men just focus on keeping the peace."

"Yes, sir."

"A hundred days, Bruce. That's all. A hundred more days and then this will all be over."

The static crackled for a few more seconds and then the recording cut out.

For a minute we sat there, trying to process what we'd just heard. Trying to make sense of something that didn't make any sense at all. My thoughts flew straight to Dad, back in Sydney. If this thing was for real...

"It's a joke, right?" said Peter way too lightly, breaking the silence. "Got to be. There's no way this is real. It's impossible."

"What's impossible?" said a curious voice from behind us.

Peter slammed his laptop shut. I spun around. Mr. Larson, our English teacher, was right behind us, eating a bagel. How long had he been standing there?

"Nothing, sir!" said Peter, a little too cheerfully. "Luke was just telling me about this movie he saw last week."

Mr. Larson raised an eyebrow. He glanced at his

watch, and then at us, clearly suspicious at the sight of three teenagers awake and ready for school with several hours to spare.

"Peter's been showing Jordan and me around town," I lied. "You know, showing us where to find everything."

"Ah, I see." Mr. Larson smiled, obviously not believing a word of it. "Well, in that case I'd better leave you to it. Good to see you being such a model citizen, Peter."

"You know me, sir, always helping!" said Peter brightly, as Mr. Larson walked off towards the school.

"Nice save," said Jordan dryly as soon as Mr. Larson was out of earshot.

I looked over at the two security guards up the street, still trying to get Crazy Bill to move along, and suddenly realized why that voice in the recording had sounded so familiar.

"The security chief!" I said.

"Huh?" said Jordan. "What about him?"

"The guy in the recording," I said. "The deep-voiced one. It's the security chief who met my mum and me when we landed here. Officer Calvin or whoever."

"Yeah, Bruce Calvin," said Peter.

"You know him?" Jordan asked.

"Sure, he's been here since the beginning," Peter said. "My dad works for him sometimes."

Jordan and I both turned to stare at him.

"Oh, come on," Peter rolled his eyes, suddenly realizing what we were thinking. "That's not – my dad has nothing to do with this!"

"How do you know?" I asked. "I mean, if that's Calvin's voice on the recording –"

"We don't know *whose* voice that is on the recording!" snapped Peter. "As if you can tell through all the static! It's probably just a couple of kids or whatever."

"A couple of kids?" Jordan said. "You think a couple of kids did all this?"

"All what?" shouted Peter, getting to his feet. "It's just talk! It could be anyone!"

"Peter, sit down!" I hissed.

"Don't tell me to –"

"Shh!" Jordan cocked her head in the direction of another nearby security guard. He'd heard Peter's shouts and was staring in our direction, like he was deciding whether or not to come over and investigate.

Peter forced his face into a smile, waved at the guard, and quickly sat down. "Look," he said, obviously struggling to stay calm, "none of this is even real, okay? It can't be. A secret plot to wipe out the human race? It's ridiculous."

"Yeah," I said, wishing I could believe that Peter was right. "Unless it's not."

"You actually think this is all happening?" said Peter, like he was going to take it as a personal insult if I said yes.

"I don't know." I stared down at the concrete. "It's not like I *want* it to be true. But we can't just ignore it."

"Sure we can," said Peter.

"No. We can't," said Jordan. She grabbed Peter's laptop and opened it in front of her. "I want to hear it again."

So we listened to the recording again. And again. And each time I heard it, the knot in my stomach pulled a little bit tighter.

But what were we supposed to do about it? If you know there's a massive global crisis about to happen, surely you go and warn the people who actually have the power to do something. You tell the prime minister or the U.N. or whatever. You don't pull a couple of random high school kids off the street and try to make it their problem.

School went by in a blur. Ms. Benson gave it to Peter for not having his embryo slide show ready to present to the class. After recess, we ditched our stuff in the gym and went out to the field to muddle our way through a game of soccer. When we got to English, Mr. Larson asked how much of *The Shape of Things to Come* we'd all read, shook his head disapprovingly at our lack of commitment, and then put on the rest of the movie.

It was a completely normal school day, but there was no room in my head for any of it. I felt like the recording on Peter's computer had swollen up and taken over my whole brain.

Bits and pieces of it kept swirling around in my mind.

Blood bath ... there won't be anyone left on the outside ... Tabitha ... human plague ... a hundred days... only create panic... Tabitha... a hundred days... cleanse the outside world... blood bath... a hundred days ...

A hundred more days and then this will all be over.

"Here's a bright idea," said Peter, snapping me out of my daze as the three of us walked across to the bike racks at the end of the day. "Why don't the two of you take the weekend off? You know, like a cooling-off period. Forget about all this end-of-the-world stuff. Then next week, if you still want to be superheroes, you can start working out your master plan."

"I dunno," I said, rifling in my bag for the key to my bike lock. "I mean, if there's even a chance that all of this is actually happening, shouldn't we –"

I stopped mid-sentence and pulled a crumpled scrap of paper from the bottom of my backpack.

"Oh, crap," said Peter.

I stared at the note. It had two sentences printed on it in big block letters, like the person who wrote it was trying to disguise their handwriting.

"It's another message from your secret admirer, isn't it?" said Peter.

THIS IS NOT A JOKE.
MEET ME AT PHOENIX AIRPORT
7 P.M. SUNDAY

Jordan snatched the note out of my hand. Peter leaned in close to read over her shoulder.

"Great," he said. "There goes my weekend."

Chapter 8

The three of us met up in front of the Phoenix Mall at lunchtime the next day. The mall wasn't exactly huge, although I guess it was okay for a town with only two thousand people. It was all on one level, with a food court at one end and a big supermarket at the other. And, of course, the whole building was completely spotless and new. You'd think I would've stopped noticing that stuff by now, but it still stuck out at me everywhere I went.

"Ninety dollars," Jordan muttered, pointing to a rack of clothes as we walked in. "What moron pays ninety dollars for a T-shirt?"

"Y-yeah," Peter agreed. He looked sideways at her and zipped up his hoodie a bit.

I stopped off at the newsstand on our way past to pick up the new issue of *Hyper*. Something normal from the outside world. But the magazine selection turned out to be pretty pathetic – only a dozen or so to pick from, plus a few copies of the *Phoenix Herald* – and I came out empty-handed.

The food court was a big round area that bulged out of the end of the building, with curved plate glass walls that made you feel like you were stuck inside a giant fish tank. The whole place was packed with kids, like any mall on a Saturday. It seemed like half of Phoenix High was employed here, busy serving pizza and sandwiches and burgers to the other half.

We grabbed some food and took our lunch to a quiet corner in the park, where we could figure out what to do about the note in my bag.

As we walked outside, I saw a truck rumbling along the wide road that ran between the mall and the medical center. It took a second to realize why the sight felt so weird to me. It was the first motor vehicle I'd seen in five days. The truck pulled to a stop outside the mall and two guys in white uniforms jumped out and started unloading big wooden crates from the back.

"Supply truck," Peter explained when he saw me staring at it. He pointed along the road that the truck had just driven down. A few blocks away, it stretched into the bush and out of sight. "That's the main road out of town, the only one that's actually big enough for a car to drive on. Trucks come in every day with supplies – you know, food and medicine and whatever."

We kept walking until we found a quiet spot out on the grass, under an enormous tree.

"I looked in the town directory," I said as we sat down. "There's no one called Tabitha anywhere in Phoenix."

"Could be an alias," said Peter through a mouthful of chips. Then, like he was agreeing with his own idea, he added, "Yeah, it'd make sense to use an alias if they're trying to keep it all under wraps."

"I thought you didn't believe any of this was true," said Jordan.

"I don't," said Peter. "But if *I* was trying to blow up the world or whatever, I'd definitely be using a fake name. Anyway, speaking of all this being made up, I asked my dad last night about the work he did for Calvin."

"What?" said Jordan, almost dropping her sandwich. "Peter, what if he –"

"Calm down," said Peter. "I didn't tell him about the recording. I just said I'd seen Calvin in town yesterday and wondered, you know, what he was like to work with."

"Smooth," said Jordan.

"What did he say?" I asked.

"He said he hardly ever deals with Calvin directly anymore, now that the security force is all set up. And even when he had actual meetings with Calvin, all he did was write up press releases and stuff for the local paper."

"So?" said Jordan.

"So even if there *was* something going on, my dad would have nothing to do with it."

"Okay, good," I said, before Jordan had time to argue. Not that any of what he'd said actually proved anything. But Peter's dad was an issue for another day.

Jordan seemed to agree. She took another bite of her sandwich and then said, "So, we're going tomorrow, right?"

"Yeah," I said, pulling the note out of my pocket and looking at it again. "Well, I want to anyway. Whoever this person is, they seem to have answers. And for some reason they want to give them to us."

"They *say* they've got answers," Peter corrected.

"Okay, whatever, but how will we know unless we go to meet them?" I said. "If it turns out that this *is* all just a load of crap, then we forget about it and move on with our lives."

"And if it's not?" said Peter, though from the tone of his voice he clearly didn't think this was a possibility.

"Dunno," I shrugged. "I guess we figure that out when we get there."

"Right," said Jordan. She turned to Peter and said, "So, are you coming or what?"

"Yeah, all right," he said, emptying the rest of his chips into his mouth. Then his eyes went wide. "Whoa, hang on. It's Larson!"

Jordan and I both spun around. "Where?"

"No, I mean your stalker guy, the one who's sending you all these messages and stuff. Five bucks says it's Mr. Larson."

"What?" said Jordan, raising an eyebrow. "Why?"

"Think about it," said Peter. "Yesterday morning, when we were listening to the recording, who just *happened* to be eavesdropping on our conversation?"

"So what?" said Jordan. "He didn't hear anything."

"Yeah, he did," Peter replied. "He heard me saying the recording wasn't real. And then, right after we came out of *his class*, we found a note saying that it *is* all real and trying to sort out a meeting."

"That's true," I said. "Mr. Larson could have slipped the note into my bag while we were watching the movie."

"What about the USBs?" asked Jordan. "Luke and I both went straight home after school on Wednesday. There's no way Mr. Larson could have made it around to both of our houses before we got back. One of us would've caught him."

Peter thought about this for a minute, obviously not wanting to give up on his theory that easily.

"Okay," he said. "All right, but who says he did it in the afternoon? What if he went and dropped them off in the morning before school started?"

"But that was before I even met him," I said, shaking my head. "It was my first day here."

"Yeah, and he already knew who you were, remember?" said Peter. "The first time you saw him, he already knew your name."

"Of course he did," said Jordan. "They'd all get told when someone new arrives. That doesn't mean anything." She scrunched up her sandwich wrapper and stuck it inside her paper cup. "Anyway, if you're still convinced that this is some big joke, why are you so worried about figuring out who's behind it?"

"Because whatever else is going on here, *someone's* sending us this stuff. And I reckon it's him."

"But why would Mr. Larson be doing it?" I asked. "It doesn't make any sense."

Peter shrugged. "Since when can you expect sense from an English teacher?" He stood up, balled up his trash, and chucked it up into the tree. "Guess we'll find out tomorrow though, won't we?"

81

Jordan and Peter rode over to my place on Sunday afternoon. We'd figured my mum would be the least likely to ask questions about where we were going and, as it turned out, she was back in the office anyway. She's never been all that clear on the concept of "weekends."

We rode out towards Phoenix Airport, backtracking along the path that Mum and I had taken into town on the night we arrived. It was only 5:30 p.m., but Jordan wanted us to get there early so we could get the jump on whoever was coming to meet us.

"Here's what I don't get," said Peter as we rode along the winding dirt path. "If you're planning a top-secret conspiracy meeting, why choose the airport? It's not the most private location, is it?"

"What if it's a setup?" I said. "A trap or something. What if Mr. Larson or whoever just wants to lure us away from the town?"

"To do what?" said Peter. "Lock us up in the departure lounge and force us to read Shakespeare?"

"That's why we're going early," said Jordan, flicking her braids out of her face. "So we can have a look around first and try to figure out what's going on."

"We need to be careful riding in," I said. "If we get there and there's a bunch of security guys –"

"Mate, it's an *airport*," Peter interrupted, looking over his shoulder at me. "What are they gonna do? It's not like we're sneaking onto private property."

I just shrugged at him and kept riding. He was probably right. But the closer we got to the airport, the edgier I got. If this *was* just some twisted joke, then whoever was behind it was clearly messed up in the head. Definitely not the kind of person I wanted to be running into on an airstrip in the middle of the bush.

And if there really was some evil psycho coverup going on, then we were riding straight into the middle of it. And there was no way that was going to end well.

"Almost there," said Peter, as we came up on the last bend in the path. "What do you guys want to do?

Just ride straight in or – whoa."

Peter skidded to a stop at the edge of the clearing, and Jordan and I pulled up behind him.

"Well," he said slowly, "doesn't look like we're going to have any trouble getting around airport security."

I looked out across the clearing. The airstrip was completely empty. All the aircraft had been flown out. The luggage carts and the refueling equipment that'd been scattered around the runway when we arrived were gone too.

There was no sign of movement anywhere. All the lights were off inside the little gray terminal building, and even from this distance I could see that everything had been bolted shut.

"Maybe they're just closed for the night," Jordan said, but I could tell from the look on her face that she didn't believe that any more than I did.

No one was coming back here in the morning.

Phoenix Airport had been completely abandoned.

Chapter 9

"You were right," I said to Peter as we wheeled our bikes out into the clearing. "Me and my mum... you said we were the last ones coming."

"This isn't exactly what I meant," said Peter, looking uneasy.

"The man in the recording said it too," said Jordan. "He called you the *final arrivals*, right?"

"Coincidence," said Peter under his breath.

The sun was starting to disappear behind the trees now, casting long, dark shadows of us and our bikes out over the tarmac. We walked across to the terminal building, and I leaned up against one of the tinted windows at the front, trying to get a look inside.

"See anything?" asked Peter.

"Nope, too dark."

Jordan walked across to the bolted front entrance. She grabbed on to the doors and shook them as hard as she could with both hands. No good. She shrugged. "Worth a shot."

"Don't worry," said Peter, digging in his pocket and pulling out a paperclip. "I got it."

He untwisted the paperclip and crouched down in front of the door, poking the little metal stick around inside the lock. He kept glancing up at Jordan out of the corner of his eye, like he wanted to make sure she was watching. But after about twenty seconds, Jordan left him to it and started walking along the length of the building, looking for another way in.

"Careful," I called out as she headed around the corner.

"Yeah," she nodded, smiling back at me before disappearing out of sight.

"Crap!" said Peter, still stooped over the front

entrance. "The end just snapped off inside."

"Do we really want to break in here?" I asked. "What if someone catches us?"

"Relax, mate," said Peter, his eyes still fixed on the keyhole. "We'll make sure we leave everything just the way we –"

SMASH!

I leapt to my feet and Peter whirled around.

Jordan was standing next to what was left of one of the windows, clutching a big stick with both hands.

"What?" she said, like what she'd just done was as normal as opening a door. She bashed the stick against the window frame a few more times, clearing the shards of glass from around the edges.

"Come on," she said, tossing the stick aside. "Let's have a look."

Peter muttered something about almost having the door unlocked, and followed Jordan through the broken window. I clambered in after them, slicing my knee on a bit of glass that was still sticking up out of the frame.

The room was pitch black, and I could only just

make out the shapes of Jordan and Peter moving in front of me. I fumbled around on the wall for a light switch, but couldn't find one.

"Guys," I whispered. "Are you sure this is a good idea?"

But the words were drowned out by a loud clunking sound. I jumped about a meter into the air as the lights suddenly flashed on all around us. Peter swore loudly. Jordan's head whooshed around, looking for the culprit.

But there was no one else there.

"Lights must be running on a sensor," said Peter, straightening up and squinting against the sudden brightness.

Breathing heavily, I stared out across the white room, wondering why it was taking my eyes so long to adjust. A second later, I figured out what the problem was.

There was nothing to see. The whole building had been emptied out.

Furniture, trash cans, vending machines – everything was gone. All that was left was a couple of marble counters concreted to the floor and the now-empty rack on the wall that had been lined with bike helmets the day we arrived.

We were silent.

I circled one of the counters, heart pounding, half-expecting to find someone lying in wait behind it.

Don't be stupid, I told myself. *This place was locked from the outside.*

On the far side of the counter was a door marked *STAFF ONLY.*

I glanced back at the others. *Try it?*

Jordan nodded.

I turned the handle and the door opened with a click. The lights switched on as I stepped inside. Nothing in there either. Just an empty wall cabinet and a couple of coffee stains on the carpet.

I walked back out into the main room, shaking my head. "I don't get it," I said in a low voice. "Why go to all the trouble of building this place if you're just going to pack up and leave it all behind?"

"Doesn't make any sense," Peter admitted.

"Definitely doesn't look like they're expecting anyone else to be coming in, does it?"

"Or out," said Jordan darkly.

Peter shrugged. "Plenty of other ways to get in and out." He walked over and looked out the window. "What's the time?"

"Quarter to seven," I said, checking the useless mobile phone I still carried with me out of habit.

"What do you reckon?" Peter asked, turning to Jordan. "Head back out and look for our stalker?"

"Yeah, let's go," she said.

I followed behind, keen to get out of there. The lights clunked off again as we left. Good. The last thing we needed right now was for someone to come and bust us for breaking and entering.

The sun had disappeared almost completely by the time we got back outside, and the bushland around us was just a blur of black. I scanned the trees, but I couldn't see any sign of –

"Look," Jordan whispered, grabbing my arm. "Over there!"

A narrow beam of light was glinting across the tarmac at the far end of the airstrip.

"A flashlight," said Peter. "That would've been a smart idea."

"Yeah," I said, suddenly realizing how stupid we'd

been not to bring any of our own.

I squinted in the direction of the flashlight, but it was impossible to tell who was out there. Whoever it was, they had to have seen us breaking into the terminal building. But they weren't coming any closer. They were just standing there, shining the flashlight around. Waiting.

"That'll be them," I said, kind of embarrassed at how shaky my voice was all of a sudden.

"Come on," said Jordan, striding out across the tarmac as though she did this sort of thing all the time.

Peter and I trailed along behind her. The end of the airstrip was further away than it looked, and the closer I got to the person with the flashlight, the more I realized that Peter wasn't the only one who'd been hoping that none of this was real.

As we closed in on our mystery informant, the beam of light suddenly swept across the airstrip and landed right on top of us.

"Hey," said Jordan irritably. "Get that out of my face!"

But the light kept shining straight at us until we

got to the end of the airstrip. We stopped about five meters away from him, and he flashed the light at each of us in turn. Then he swung it around, lighting up his own face like he was about to tell us a ghost story.

I rubbed my eyes, still half-blind from the light.

It was Crazy Bill.

Chapter 10

"You?" said Peter, like there'd been a mistake.

Crazy Bill grinned, his disfigured face scrunching up like a piece of paper. He bent over and put his flashlight down on the ground between us so that we could see each other clearly. With a grunt, he straightened up again and stared at Jordan and me.

I tried not to breathe in too deeply. It was painfully obvious that Bill still hadn't washed since the last time we'd seen him.

"Knew you'd bring him," he said, pointing at Peter. His voice was harsh and gravelly, like whatever had scarred him on the outside had damaged his insides as well.

"What's that supposed to mean?" Peter asked, his nose crinkling slightly.

Crazy Bill grunted again. He threw back his shoulders and gritted his teeth, and for a second I thought he was going to take a swing at Peter.

Then he slouched back down and started muttering to himself. "Yes, yes. It's always the same."

I took a couple of steps back. This guy was clearly unhinged.

"Why don't you tell us why you brought us here?" Jordan asked in a slow, gentle, talking-to-crazy-people voice. "What did you want to talk to us about?"

Crazy Bill turned to look at Jordan, but didn't say anything. His eyes sort of glazed over and I couldn't tell if he was figuring out an answer or if he just hadn't heard the question.

A minute went by in silence.

"Wait a sec," said Peter. "If this was you all along – how did you deliver those messages in the first place? How did you get into our houses?"

Bill snapped out of his daze. "Used a key," he said impatiently, as though this should have been obvious.

"Needed to bring them together." He stretched out his hands to point at Jordan and me.

"Why us?" I asked. "Out of all the people – I mean, if there's something going on here, then you need to tell someone who can actually fix it!"

"*You* need to fix it!" Crazy Bill barked. "Both of you. Together. I need your help."

"You need *their* help to save the world?" said Peter, sounding offended that the smelly homeless man was leaving him out of his plans.

"No," said Bill. "Not the world. First, you help me."

"Help you do what?" asked Jordan.

Crazy Bill went quiet again. He let out another long, gruff sigh and put his face down in his filthy hands. When he finally spoke, it sounded like he might be about to cry.

"Please, I n-need –" he said, the words catching in his throat. "It's almost t-time. This is not – this is non-n-negotiable! I need to leave – I need to go back!"

"Go back where?" asked Jordan softly. She stuck her arm out a bit, and then held it in midair, like she was debating whether she could bring herself to actually reach out and comfort him.

"Hang on," Peter cut in, "what about the recording you sent us? If you're saying it's real –"

"Of course it's real," Bill snapped.

"Well, shouldn't that be our first priority then?" Peter asked. "Assuming you have any proof that this is actually happening. If we've only got a hundred days before Tabitha blows up the world or whatever –"

"Ninety-four," Bill corrected him, "point two."

Peter stared at him for a second. "Uh, okay. Whatever. What I'm saying is that if there's really some massive global threat out there, then shouldn't we deal with that first before we worry about getting you a plane ticket back to wherever it is you've –?"

Crazy Bill let out a sudden howl of frustration that stopped Peter mid-sentence. He screwed up his face and gnashed his teeth like this whole conversation was causing him physical pain. Peter leapt back, ready to run for it if he had to. I stood there, rooted to the spot.

Bill clenched and unclenched his fists a couple of times. He took a deep breath, recovered himself, and said, "If I provide the evidence, if I answer your questions, will you agree to help me?"

"Of course," said Jordan.

"Okay," said Crazy Bill wearily, running a hand through his greasy hair. "Okay then."

Silence fell again. Bill looked back and forth between Jordan and me.

"All right," I said, when it seemed like no one else was going to say anything. "Well, for a start, who's Tabitha? The recording you gave us said something about someone called…"

I trailed off. Crazy Bill was shooting me an irritated look, like he couldn't believe I was wasting his time with such a stupid question.

"No, that's not right," he said, pacing like a caged animal. "But you haven't found – no. No, that's not what you should be asking. It's not –"

Suddenly, there was a burst of light from behind us. Crazy Bill held up his hands to shield his face.

I spun around. Four men in black uniforms were coming towards us, flashlights in hand.

Officer Calvin and his security staff.

Chapter 11

Crazy Bill's eyes went wide.

"Run for it?" I hissed.

"Too late," said Peter. "They've already seen us."

My eyes flashed down to Calvin's right hand, which was hovering over the gun holstered to his side. How much had he heard?

Suddenly, Crazy Bill was pacing again. He started muttering under his breath, words coming out in a rush like he was hurrying to say it all before it was too late. It was so incoherent that I could only pick up bits of it.

"Fury — met in the house — both go to law —"

"What?" said Peter. "Mate, what are you talking about?"

But then Calvin cut into the middle of our circle, putting himself between us and Crazy Bill. "Step away from him please, children," he ordered, as the other three men fanned out around Bill.

Crazy Bill took a step forward. *"I will prosecute you!"* he shouted, spattering spit across Calvin's face.

The Chief stood his ground, fingers brushing the grip of his pistol.

"He tricked us, chief!" said Peter quickly. "Crazy Bill –"

"*Now* please, children," said Calvin, shooting a quick glance back over his shoulder. "Out of the way. He could be dangerous."

My eyes darted between Officer Calvin and Crazy Bill. I backed away, not wanting to mess with either of them. Jordan and Peter did the same, but we all stopped moving as soon as Calvin turned his back.

"Come, I'll take no denial!" Crazy Bill was babbling. *"We must have the trial –"*

"Now, now," said Calvin, hand slowly closing around his gun, "no one's talking about a trial. We just need you to come away from these children and –"

"– *really, this morning I've nothing to do!*" Bill shouted him down.

"Reeve," Calvin said urgently, waving a hand in our direction, "get them out of here."

"Yes, sir," said one of the guards, immediately moving towards us, while the other two circled around behind Crazy Bill.

"*Such a trial, dear sir, with no jury or judge –*"

"C'mon," said Reeve, putting a hand on my shoulder. "Time to go."

"*– wasting our breath!*"

"Who *is* that guy?" I asked, still not taking my eyes away from Crazy Bill as the guard ushered us away.

"He's just a street crazy," said Reeve. "Usually doesn't give us any trouble, but if he's luring kids out here at night –"

"*I'll be judge!*" Crazy Bill shouted at the top of his lungs. "*I'll be jury!*"

"Those your bikes over there?" Reeve asked, ignoring Bill and shining his flashlight over at the terminal.

"Huh? Oh. Yeah," I said, glancing back over my shoulder as we headed towards the gray building. The guards behind Crazy Bill had both drawn their weapons. Bill turned to look at one of them. He froze on the spot. But there was no fear in his eyes, just a kind of crazed determination.

"I'll try the whole cause!" he raved.

"That's enough," said Calvin firmly, training his own weapon on Crazy Bill. "If you cannot control yourself, I will be forced to –"

"I'll try the whole cause and condemn you to DEATH!"

"See?" Reeve told us. "Complete head case. But we'll bring him back to the station and make sure he gets –"

There was a shout behind us, followed by a loud "OOF!" as someone got tackled to the ground. Looking back, I could just make out two people wrestling on the tarmac.

"Nothing to worry about," Reeve said anxiously, hurrying us along. "All under control."

BLAM!

One of the other security guards had opened fire.

Crazy Bill let out a growl: hurt, or maybe just angry.

"Get down!" Reeve ordered, spinning around.

The three of us dropped to the ground, but there was no cover anywhere. Nothing to hide behind. Just flat tarmac all the way out to the bush. All it would take was for one stray bullet to come whizzing our way and –

BLAM! BLAM!

If you've never heard gunfire up close, you've got no idea how terrifying it is. I imagined every one of those bullets ripping a hole straight through me.

I raised my head slightly, trying to catch sight of what was going on through the officers' flashlight beams, but they were moving around so much that it was almost impossible to make anything out. I heard more shouts and the sound of footsteps on gravel, and then Crazy Bill howled like an animal.

"Chief!" someone shouted. "Quick, grab his –"

A panicked scream cut across the airstrip, and one of the flashlights went clattering to the ground. The screaming quickly got louder and I saw something big and solid-looking shooting through the air, headed straight for us. I dived out of the way just in time to avoid being flattened by the flying mass as it hit the ground. There was a sickening crunch and the screaming stopped.

Jordan gasped. Peter made a gagging noise. I rolled over on the tarmac and felt a massive shudder rip through my body. A single, bulging, bloodshot eye was staring back at me, inches from my face.

It was one of the guards. He'd hit the ground face-first and his arms were splayed out at his sides, bending at angles that arms are definitely not supposed to bend at. I fought back a scream, scrambled away from him and jumped to my feet. The eye kept staring for a few seconds, then rolled back up into its socket.

"Weary!" Reeve shouted, shoving me aside and bending down to check the man's pulse. "Are you –?"

BLAM!

Dropping to the ground again, I heard footsteps thundering closer. Someone running towards us. There was a thud and another crunch of gravel and the runner was knocked down onto the tarmac.

BLAM! BLAM! BLAM!

The gunshots were closer this time, more frantic.

"Put it away!" Calvin ordered. "You're only making him –"

His voice turned into a scream and I saw another dark shape go flying across the tarmac.

I turned away, shuddering, as Calvin thudded to the ground.

Officer Reeve stood up again, looking pale in the flashlight's beam. He froze, probably trying to decide whether to stay with us or go back.

There was another volley of gunshots.

Jordan's eyes flashed to Reeve. "Should we –?"

"No," he said. "Go. Get out of here, fast as you can. Go *straight home*."

"Definitely," Peter said, sounding like he was about to be sick.

Officer Reeve tossed me his flashlight and then ran back to join the fray.

We ran the rest of the way to the terminal building, grabbed our bikes, and pedaled away down the dirt track into the bush.

Chapter 12

There was no sign of Crazy Bill anywhere in town the next day.

Not that I was expecting to see him. If he'd escaped the guards, he'd probably be hiding out somewhere, lying low. Or else he'd been shot or arrested, in which case he definitely wouldn't be roaming the streets anytime soon.

I'd fallen asleep as soon as my head hit the pillow last night, but it didn't last long. My dreams were a mess of shouts and gunshots and flashes of Crazy Bill's twisted face, and I kept jolting awake, half-expecting to find that poor security officer's crumpled body still lying next to me, his huge unblinking eye drilling a hole in my head.

It was almost a relief when my alarm finally got me up for school.

I saw Jordan on the way there. She was walking out of the office complex as I rode past, through a glass sliding door marked Phoenix Medical Center. She waved to me on her way down the steps and I stopped to wait for her.

"Everything okay?" I asked as she came over.

"Huh?" She followed my eyes back to the medical center. "Oh, right. Yeah, everything's fine. Mum just went in for an appointment. Nothing serious."

"Oh, okay. Good."

"I got up early to come in with her," Jordan continued, bending down to unlock her bike from a rack out in front of the building. "You know, as a peace offering after last night. She wasn't too happy when I came home after dark without a good reason."

"But it was only eight-thirty!" I said, raising an eyebrow. "Besides, it's not like you could have called her and told her where you were."

"Yeah, but missing dinner without a good reason

is basically a criminal offense in my family," said Jordan, standing up again. "What about you? How was your mum about it?"

"She doesn't even know I was gone," I said as we wheeled our bikes back out onto the street. "I beat her home by twenty minutes."

"Lucky," said Jordan.

"I guess so," I shrugged. But as far as family problems went, I thought having a mum who wanted me home in time for dinner was probably not so terrible.

We walked down the street in silence for a while. I was still lost in the insanity of the night before, and I figured Jordan was probably feeling the same. She had this steely look in her eyes, like she was trying to push it all down so she didn't have to think about it. I felt like I should say something to her. Ask her how she was feeling, or reassure her that everything would be okay, or ... I don't know. Something. But I couldn't find the words for any of it.

In the end, she was the one to break the silence.

"At least the security people haven't contacted our parents," she said.

"Yeah," I said. "Not yet, anyway."

Jordan looked thoughtful. "I don't think they will. Whatever Calvin is planning, the other guy in the recording told him to keep it quiet. I don't think he'll want to draw any unnecessary attention to what happened out there last night."

"Yeah, guess not."

"Assuming any of them even made it back from the airport," Jordan added quietly.

My mind flashed back to Crazy Bill's sudden psychopathic outburst, to that dark shape curving through the air towards me, to that horrible screaming that got louder and louder and then suddenly *stopped*.

"You saw it, right?" I said, after a minute.

"Saw what?"

"That security guard last night. The one who, you know, crashed into the ground next to us. He was – I mean, it *looked* like…"

"It looked like Crazy Bill chucked him through the air," Jordan supplied.

"But that can't be what actually happened, right?" I said, trying to stay rational. "No one has that kind of –"

"Look!" said Jordan suddenly, pointing across the street.

It took me a minute to figure out who she was looking at. Officer Reeve was walking up the steps to the security center, dressed in a T-shirt and jeans instead of his normal security gear. He looked pretty messed up, but at least he was still standing.

"Do you reckon we should go over?" I asked.

But Jordan was already running to catch up with Reeve before he got inside. "Officer Reeve!" she called, ditching her bike on the grass outside the building.

Reeve stopped and turned around. One of his arms was bound up in plaster and the other one was covered in some nasty-looking grazes. He had bruising all across his face and about twenty stitches holding his cheek together. Seeing him in daylight, I realized he wasn't all that much older than we were – he only looked about twenty-five.

"Oh, g'day," he said to us, coming back down the stairs. "You kids get home all right last night?"

"Yeah," said Jordan. "Thanks."

Reeve smiled, and then winced at the pain in his face.

"You okay?" I asked, trying not to cringe.

"Seem to be," said Reeve. "Looks worse than it feels. Doc Montag's given me a few days off though, to be on the safe side. Just coming in to deliver a statement and then I'm heading home."

"And the others?" Jordan pressed. "Are they...?"

Officer Reeve's smile disappeared. "They copped it worse than I did," he said grimly. "From what I've heard, they reckon the chief should be back on his feet before long, but the others..." Reeve gazed back over the road at the medical center and let out a sigh. "Officer Weary didn't make it."

I gaped at him, horrified. Obviously it hadn't looked good for the security guard, but realizing that I'd just seen someone *die* right in front of me... I shuddered.

Reeve nodded sadly. Then, like he was forcing himself to stay positive, he straightened up and said, "They're still working on Lazzaro, though. If anyone can sort him out, Doc Montag can."

I glanced sideways at Jordan and she raised an eyebrow.

"What about Crazy Bill?" I asked carefully. "Did

you catch him?"

"Oh," said Reeve, not quite making eye contact. "We're, uh, not really at liberty to discuss that at the moment. We're still in the middle of our investigation and…" he trailed off again, looking down at his watch. Then, suddenly cheerful, he added, "Anyway, I'd better let you two get going. Wouldn't want you to be late for school. You kids stay out of trouble, all right?"

"Uh, right," I said. "See you."

Officer Reeve gave us another wincing smile and made his way back up the stairs.

"Crazy Bill got away," said Peter knowingly, when we told him about running into Reeve. "He definitely got away."

We were sitting in our science class threading beads onto bits of string. In theory, we were supposed to be modeling polypeptide synthesis. But in reality, most people were just making necklaces or chucking the beads at each other when Ms. Benson wasn't looking.

With all of that going on, we figured it was safe enough to continue our conversation, as long as we sat at the back and kept our voices down.

"How do you know?" Jordan whispered.

"Because," said Peter impatiently, "if they *had* caught him, Officer Reeve would've said so. Besides, no way were Calvin's guys ever going to come out on top in that fight. All the way out at the airport with two men down already and no way to call for – *ow!*"

Across the room, I could see Michael and Tank laughing. One of them had just chucked over a bead and nailed Peter right in the eye.

Peter grabbed a bead from our table and stood up to return fire.

"Peter!" said Ms. Benson sternly from the front.

"I was just stretching, miss!" said Peter, looking scandalized.

"You can stretch on your own time. Right now you've got work to do," said Ms. Benson.

"Yes, miss." Peter sat down again. He made an obscene hand gesture at the other table and then turned his attention back to our conversation.

"I just don't get how the security guards were so quick to find us last night," Jordan said in a low voice, once Ms. Benson had looked away. "They had no reason to suspect us, did they?"

"Can't have," said Peter. "Wouldn't have let us go if they did."

"Maybe they knew Crazy Bill was dangerous," I suggested. "If they knew about his, you know, super strength, then maybe they –"

I stopped at the smirk on Peter's face. "What?"

"Mate, you just used the words *super strength* like you thought that was something a person in the real world could actually *have*."

"You saw what he did last night!" I blurted, drawing a glare from Ms. Benson. "What, you think that security guy just –"

"I don't know *what* I saw last night," Peter insisted, "but if Calvin and his mates thought Bill was that dangerous, why have they been letting him roam the streets all this time?"

"I think most of them are just doing what they're told," said Jordan. "Calvin's obviously on edge, but I don't think the rest of them know what's really going on here."

"And we do?" asked Peter.

"We know more than they do, at least," Jordan

told him. "Officer Reeve was way too casual talking to us back there to actually be working with Calvin. I think he probably gave away more than –"

Jordan stopped short, seeing Ms. Benson walking towards us. We all made a show of being hard at work with our beads. I turned last night over in my head yet again, trying to come up with an explanation that didn't involve superpowers.

"All right," I said, when she was back out of earshot, "so maybe Calvin didn't know about Crazy Bill's … *special abilities,* or whatever you want to call them. Maybe it's not about that. What if they were out there last night because Calvin figured out Bill knew something about Tabitha?"

"Why'd they just let us go home then?" said Peter. "If Calvin's so worried about being exposed or whatever, why haven't they hauled us three off to –?"

There was a knock on the door and another teacher walked into the room. She was a dumpy-looking woman I didn't recognize, with short brown hair and a big mole on her chin.

"Uh-oh," said Peter. "Pryor."

"The principal?" I asked.

"No," said Peter, rolling his eyes, "the astronaut."

Ms. Pryor walked across to Ms. Benson and whispered something in her ear. Ms. Benson nodded and cleared her throat. "Peter, Jordan and Luke, would you come here for a moment? Ms. Pryor would like a word with you in her office."

Chapter 13

"Busted!" Tank called with a grin as the three of us
filed out after Ms. Pryor.

Peter gave him the finger again as he walked out
the door.

"I saw that, Peter!" Ms. Benson warned.

"Sorry, miss!"

We followed Ms. Pryor across the school in
silence. Clearly this wasn't a coincidence – the school
principal suddenly here, suddenly wanting to talk
to us. Someone must have told her about last night.
Had Calvin figured out what we were really up to?
Was this just a handover? Was Ms. Pryor just taking

us to the front office so we could get picked up and dragged away by security?

I looked questioningly at Peter, but he just shook his head and mouthed, *Play dumb.*

A couple of Year 7 girls poked their heads out of a second-floor window as we walked past.

"Back inside, please, ladies," said Ms. Pryor, smiling up at them. "I'm sure you have plenty of work to be getting on with."

The heads disappeared again.

I stared at Ms. Pryor, trying to get a read on her. She seemed friendly enough, but there was something about her that gave me the feeling she couldn't be trusted. It was almost like she reminded me of someone, but I couldn't figure out whether it was just the usual principal creepiness, or … something else.

Ms. Pryor led us across the quad and up the stairs to the front office. Without saying a word, she rounded a corner, strode down the narrow hallway, and stopped at a steel door with no handle.

She pulled out a card and waved it front of a sensor on the doorjamb. There was a clunk as the door unlocked, and she pushed it open, motioning for us to go inside. I felt like I was being ushered into a prison cell. Seriously, what principal needs that kind of security?

Pryor's office was small and cramped, but it still had that too-perfect vibe I was getting so familiar with in Phoenix. Everything was neatly arranged. An enormous red and gold rug stretched out across the floor, half-covered by a wooden writing desk that was probably an antique. Two identical vases of flowers sat on little pedestal things, one on each side of the desk. They gave the room this weird symmetrical look, like it had been designed by a robot.

Behind Pryor's desk was a tapestry that took up nearly the whole wall. It was a picture of a green field filled with enormous trees, wildflowers and wild animals, with rolling hills in the background and a big golden sun. I thought maybe it was supposed to be a picture of the Garden of Eden.

The whole room was creepy and foreboding, which I guess is half the point of a principal's office, but at least there was no sign of Calvin's men.

There was another clunk as Ms. Pryor pulled the

door shut behind us. She smoothed down the hem of her suit jacket, took a seat at her desk and waved a hand at a row of three chairs on the opposite side. We sat down.

Ms. Pryor reached across her desk and opened the laptop that was sitting there. She leaned forward and clicked the mouse a few times, clearly not in any hurry to get started, almost like she was enjoying keeping us twisted in suspense. She obviously wanted to make it very clear who was in control here. Like we needed reminding.

Pryor lifted her hand up from the keyboard, made a tiny adjustment to her screen, then sat back in her chair again and finally opened her mouth to speak. "Thank you for coming," she said, as if we'd had any choice. "Mr. Hunter, Miss Burke, it's a pleasure to finally meet you both. I'm very much looking forward to seeing what you can achieve as part of our family here in Phoenix."

That's what Mr. Ketterley had called us on the night we arrived. A family.

I stared at Pryor. The more I got to know this

"family," the less I wanted anything to do with—

Then I realized with a jolt who Pryor reminded me of.

Right after Dad moved out, Mum decided it would be a good idea for me to get some counseling. It was a plan that lasted exactly one session and was probably the worst in her long line of misguided attempts to deal with the fallout from the divorce without *actually* dealing with it.

The counselor she'd stuck me with was this smiley-faced woman who went to great pains to convince me that the two of us were going to be best friends. But clearly it was all a joke. Deep down we both knew she was getting paid to serve someone else's agenda.

And right now I was getting exactly the same vibe from Ms. Pryor.

"My apologies for not being very visible at school lately," she went on. "I've been incredibly snowed under with one thing and another."

"Oh," I said, aware that she was looking right at me. "Right. No worries."

"I trust you've had no trouble settling in?"

"No, Ms. Pryor," said Jordan, shifting slightly in her seat. "Everyone's been really helpful."

"Excellent. Yes, I've been told that Mr. Weir in particular has taken it upon himself to show the two of you around."

"Just doing my job, miss," Peter grinned.

Pryor's expression didn't budge, and I had to wonder whether Peter's usual talking-to-teachers charm had met its match.

"Indeed," she said. "However, Mr. Weir, while I'm pleased that you're displaying such a selfless attitude, I must say that I'm disappointed with some of the locations you've elected to explore."

"Sorry?" said Peter, his grin faltering.

"I have become aware, for instance, of the excursion the three of you took to Phoenix Airport last night."

Surprise flashed across Peter's face.

Ms. Pryor smiled back at him. "There are no secrets in Phoenix, Mr. Weir."

Her eyes shifted across to her computer screen,

and then back to us. "I must admit," she said, her voice suddenly cooler, "that I am more than a little concerned by this behavior."

"Concerned, miss?" said Peter innocently.

"Yes, Mr. Weir," Ms. Pryor said firmly. "I am concerned that three otherwise intelligent members of the Phoenix High School community allowed themselves to be lured away by a man who, quite honestly, should never have been permitted to set foot in this town in the first place. Have you any explanation for this extremely foolhardy behavior?"

"No, Ms. Pryor," Peter mumbled, staring at the floor. He'd clearly had a lot of practice acting remorseful in front of teachers.

"None of you?" Ms. Pryor pressed.

Jordan and I shook our heads. Pryor's eyes bore into us. How much had she actually been told about last night?

"This man – whom I believe you have been calling Crazy Bill – is a disturbed and dangerous individual." She gave a little shudder, like she was thinking of something horrible. "Thank goodness

Officer Calvin found you out there," she added heavily. "I hate to think what might've happened to you if he hadn't come through to check on the refurbishments to the airport!"

"Refurbishments, Ms. Pryor?" said Jordan earnestly, almost matching Peter for acting ability.

"Surely you must have wondered why the whole area had been vacated?" she said, raising an eyebrow. "Phoenix Airport's facilities have never been quite on par with the rest of the town, and Mr. Shackleton has just commissioned a building project to bring them up to scratch."

"Oh," said Jordan, nodding thoughtfully. "That makes sense."

Of course, it didn't really make any sense at all. I fought to keep my face expressionless, but my mind was rushing to poke holes through her story. So Calvin just *happened* to be wandering through at the same time we were meeting with Crazy Bill? Backed up by three armed guards? In the middle of the night? To check on refurbishments to an airport that was already brand new?

It was ridiculous. But right now, I knew the smartest thing to do was pretend to swallow whatever Ms. Pryor wanted to feed us.

She stared at each of us in turn, like she was trying to figure out whether we'd bought her story. Then she leaned forward in her seat, pressed her fingertips together, and said, "I'd like you to tell me what he said to you."

The temperature in the office suddenly dropped about ten degrees.

"What?" said Peter. "I mean, excuse me, miss?"

"The homeless man," Ms. Pryor said. Her eyes flickered to her laptop again, and I had the sudden suspicion that she was recording our conversation. "What did he say to you last night, out at the airport?"

"Nothing," said Jordan, a little too quickly.

Ms. Pryor raised an eyebrow. "Nothing?"

I cringed as Jordan's expression flickered.

"Nothing worth hearing," Peter jumped in. "Like you said, miss, he's crazy. Most of it was just ranting. You know, the government stealing his thoughts and all that."

Ms. Pryor stared at Peter, right into his eyes, like she was trying to steal *his* thoughts. Peter stared back, his face completely blank.

"I see," she said. "Well, *whatever* he said, I'm sure I don't need to tell you that they were only the schizophrenic ravings of a paranoid delusional. Paying them any attention would be a mistake."

"Right," said Peter. "Unless we want to learn how to make a helmet to protect ourselves from the mind control beams."

Ms. Pryor's nostrils flared slightly. "Curiosity is a slippery slope. I would advise the three of you to tread more carefully in the future if you do not wish to bring trouble upon yourselves. I'm sure that it goes without saying how *extremely* upset I will be if I hear any further reports of such reckless behavior. Is that clear?"

"Yes, Ms. Pryor," we said together.

"Wonderful," she said, suddenly friendly again. She stood up and came around to shake each of our hands. "I really am so glad that we're all understanding each other."

She unbolted her office door and ushered us back outside.

125

As soon as we got back out into the quad, Peter let out a massive sigh of relief. I guess as far as he was concerned, we'd wriggled out of trouble and that was the end of it.

But at that moment, I was feeling anything but relieved. And from the look on Jordan's face, she'd come to the exact same conclusion as me.

Pryor had told us a whole lot more than she'd meant to back there. The whole point of that conversation had obviously been to convince us that Crazy Bill was not to be trusted, and to explain away every suspicious thing we'd seen last night. And as far as I could see, there was only one reason Pryor would do all that.

Everything Crazy Bill had shown us so far – the abandoned airport, the recorded message, the plot to kill everyone outside of Phoenix…

It was all real. Every last stomach-churning bit.

And Ms. Pryor knew it.

Chapter 14

The next morning, we found out just how serious Ms. Pryor was about putting a stop to our "reckless behavior."

I got to school right on the bell and ran into Peter at the bike racks.

"C'mon," he said as I finished chaining up my bike. "We're all meant to go to the hall in period one."

"What for?"

"Dunno. Special assembly or something."

"Oh. Well, at least we get out of history," I said. "Couple more days for you to rewrite that essay for Mr. Hanger, right?"

"Nope," said Peter, gritting his teeth. "Ran into the Hanger about five minutes ago. Told me not to think I was getting an extension just because we were missing his class. He wants the new essay by the end of the day."

"Are you going to do it?" I asked as we walked off towards the hall.

"Yeah, right," said Peter. "I'll just print off another copy of the old one and hand that in again. As if he's gonna notice."

We found Jordan in the crowd of kids pushing their way towards the theatre, and the three of us made our way inside.

"You guys know what this is about?" she asked.

I shook my head. "Do you think maybe –?"

"Hang on," Peter interrupted as I started sidling into the back row after Jordan, "let's get seats in the middle."

"Huh?"

"Well, if you still reckon Pryor thinks we're up to something," Peter said, "wouldn't it be better to sit down there somewhere, instead of hiding at the back looking all secretive?"

"Yeah, good thinking," said Jordan, and we moved back into the aisle to find some seats closer to the front.

It *was* good thinking, but seeing as Peter was still convinced the two of us were just being paranoid, I didn't get why he was the one suggesting it.

But then, as Jordan stopped at three empty seats halfway down the room, Peter sidestepped in front of me and took my place next to her.

I shook my head and turned my attention to the stage. So far, there was no one down there, and even the chairs that had been set up for our last assembly were missing.

"I was talking to my mum last night," said Jordan, her voice low. "You know how she went to the medical center yesterday? She said that in the middle of her appointment, Calvin burst into the room, all bloody and bruised, and demanded to see the doctor."

"About what?" said Peter, putting his feet up on the seat in front of him.

"Apparently, the nurses weren't letting him out," said Jordan. "They wanted to keep him there for a couple of days – you know, to monitor his injuries. But Mum said Calvin was totally determined to leave. He said he didn't have time to waste lying around in hospital beds when there was a security risk on the loose."

"Crazy Bill," said Peter. "Told you he got away."

"So did they let him out?" I asked.

"Dunno," said Jordan. "The doctor got up right away and asked Mum to leave. He said they'd need to reschedule her appointment."

"Seriously?" I said. "Is he even allowed to do that?"

"Well, Mum wasn't happy, but what was she going to do about it? They've booked her in again for tomorrow," said Jordan.

"Weird," said Peter. "But, hey, at least you two don't have all that end-of-the-world stuff to worry about anymore, right?"

"What are you talking about?" said Jordan.

"Well, now that Pryor's pretty much explained it all. Got to admit, she made a lot more sense than –"

"You actually *believed* that crap?" said Jordan, almost pityingly.

Peter's eyes flashed and I could tell he had a biting

response ready to roll out. But, because it was Jordan, he took a second to reword it into something gentler.

"Look, I'm not saying I one-hundred-percent agree with everything Pryor told us back there, but what's more believable: her story about the airport getting upgraded or the crazy hobo's tale of a secret evil plan to blow up the human race?"

It might have been a fair enough question if someone else had asked it. But I got the feeling Peter's disbelief was less about what was harder to explain and more about what he *wanted* to be true.

"Think about it," he continued when he could see that neither of us was convinced. "Crazy Bill comes along with this mysterious doomsday warning, but then he drags us out to the airport and we find out he doesn't even want to talk about it. He just wants us to help *him* get out of town or whatever. Don't you think it's possible that he made the whole thing up to get us to help him?"

"Kind of a roundabout way of asking for our help, isn't it?" I said, bringing my voice down to a whisper as a group of girls shuffled into the seats in front of us.

"What about Crazy Bill's recording?" said Jordan. "He made that up too, did he?"

"I've been telling you from the start that it's a fake," said Peter. "Anyone with a bit of digital editing experience could have –"

"Right," Jordan muttered, "because Crazy Bill is *definitely* a massive computer nerd."

Peter looked like he'd love to keep arguing, but I guess he could see that Jordan was starting to get fired up because he dropped it. The hall continued to fill up around us, and my mind drifted back to our meeting with Crazy Bill.

"Here's what I don't get," I said, after a minute. "Out at the airport – when we first got there – Crazy Bill was *almost* making sense. I mean, not that I had any idea what he was talking about half the time, but he was at least sort of coherent. But then security rocks up and he just loses it – launches into all that stuff about his trial and how he's going to prosecute Calvin."

"Yeah," said Peter, nodding. "Anyone else reckon all that sounded familiar?"

Jordan and I both stared at him.

"Okay," said Peter. "I'm gonna take that as a no."

We heard footsteps echoing down on the stage and looked over to see who it was.

"Good morning, everyone," Ms. Pryor said warmly.

Some of the younger kids started chorusing "Good morning" back to her, but she steamrolled right over the top of them.

"I don't wish to keep you from your classes any longer than necessary, so I'll be brief. We have a guest this morning who's requested a few minutes of our time to make an important announcement concerning student safety. Please welcome Officer Bruce Calvin, Chief of Phoenix Security."

A few people clapped, but the applause was drowned out by gasps and whispers as Calvin made his way onto the stage.

He looked terrible, even worse than Officer Reeve. The whole left side of his body was being held together by a mess of stitches and bandages, and most of his face was covered in one huge bruise. His nose was bent out of shape, his right leg was in plaster, and he hobbled out from behind the curtain on a crutch.

It looked like even moving across the stage was a big effort. Calvin stopped at the lectern and swayed slightly, like he might be about to lose his balance.

"That will do," said Ms. Pryor sternly, and the noise in the theatre died down again.

"Thank you," said Calvin, managing to sound strong and commanding despite his injuries. "It's a pleasure to be here at Phoenix High, and I only wish I were visiting under happier circumstances."

The school was silent now, all eyes fixed on Calvin, though I assumed most of them were just hoping his announcement would include the story of how he got those injuries.

"Phoenix is a town that prides itself on providing its citizens with the highest possible standard of safety," Calvin went on, gripping the lectern for support. "And, as I'm sure you all know, my role as Chief of Security is to ensure that this standard is upheld. Unfortunately, there is one Phoenix resident who seems intent on disrupting the peaceful way of life we've been working so hard to maintain."

Calvin tapped a button on the lectern and a giant photo of Crazy Bill appeared on the projector screen behind him. For a few seconds, everyone started whispering again, but they all stopped as soon as Calvin opened his mouth.

"Many of you will have seen this man wandering the streets of Phoenix. Until recently, my security staff and I considered him to be perfectly harmless. However, we now know this *Crazy Bill* to be an extremely dangerous individual capable of –" Calvin's face twisted into a wince, "– *violent* outbursts."

Calvin tapped at the lectern again and the image behind him disappeared.

"Rest assured that my security team is working around the clock to track this criminal down and bring him to justice," he boomed. "In the meantime, I have spoken to your principal and, between us, we have decided on an appropriate next step in ensuring the safety of all Phoenix High students."

Murmurs began to fill the theatre again.

"Beginning tonight," Calvin pushed on over the noise, "Phoenix will be imposing a curfew on all persons under the age of eighteen. For as long as this curfew stands, no student will be permitted to leave their home after dark unless they are under the supervision of a parent or guardian." Calvin's eyes swept the hall, like he was searching for someone.

"Any student in breach of this curfew will be brought directly to the Phoenix Security Center, where they will have *me* to answer to. And I can assure you –" his eyes froze, suddenly fixed on the three of us, "– the consequences of such disobedience will not be pleasant."

Chapter 15

"Did you see the way Calvin was staring us down back there?" I said as we left the hall. The vague feeling I'd had of being watched all week suddenly had a name and a face. "It was almost like he was daring us to put a foot out of line, just so he could have an excuse to come after us."

"You reckon?" said Peter. "I mean, yeah, he was trying to scare us. But he was trying to scare everybody. Parading around on stage like that, showing off his injuries to the whole world – perfect way to make sure no one goes anywhere near Crazy Bill."

"Right," said Jordan. "He suspects us, obviously,

but so far all he knows is that we've had one conversation with Crazy Bill at the airport."

Technically, there were still about fifteen minutes left of our history period, but it didn't seem like anyone was exactly rushing off to class. We found a place to sit out on the grass. Peter opened his laptop and got to work changing the fonts in his essay for Mr. Hanger to make it look like he'd rewritten it.

"It definitely proves Bill's got them on edge, though," said Jordan. "Putting a curfew on the whole school because of *one* missing person who's never even attacked a student? Not exactly standard procedure, is it?"

I'd had the exact same thought. "Doubt it," I said. "Although I think standard procedure pretty much goes out the window when you're plotting to –"

I stopped short as Cathryn, Tank and Michael came past. They were obviously in the middle of an argument, although it was hard to tell how serious any of them were about it.

"C'mon, Mike," said Cathryn, thrusting an open hand out in front of him. "Pay up."

"*No*," he said, rolling his eyes and pushing the

hand away. "Look, I told you, it doesn't count."

"As if it doesn't!" said Tank.

"I said Pryor would run the assembly *this week*," said Cathryn, flicking her blonde hair indignantly. "And she did. So hand over the money."

"There wasn't even supposed to *be* an assembly today," Michael protested.

"Yeah?" said Cathryn. "Well, turns out there was one. So are you going to give me my five bucks or do I have to –?"

"Oi, Peter!" Michael yelled, spotting the three of us. "Tell Cat that didn't count as a real assembly!"

Cathryn looked over and narrowed her eyes at Peter. "Why are you bringing *him* into it?" she said coldly. "He's not even –"

"Not even *what?*" Peter challenged her.

Cathryn stared at him, then turned away like she was going to walk off.

"No, come on," said Peter, moving his laptop and getting to his feet. "You've got a problem with me? Let's hear it."

"Problem?" said Cathryn, whirling around again. "Just because you've randomly decided to start

139

ditching your real friends to hang out with these two losers you don't even know? No, Peter, why would I have a problem with that?"

"Screw you," Peter sneered. "You want to talk about ditching friends? How about the three of you disappearing after school every day and leaving me to –"

"It's not like that," said Cathryn, gritting her perfect teeth.

"No?" said Peter angrily. "What's it like then?"

Cathryn opened her mouth to respond, but Michael glared at her and she closed it again.

Peter stood staring at them for a minute, then shook his head and said, "You know what? Forget it."

He sat back down on the grass, fuming, and picked up his laptop.

"What was all that about?" I asked as the three of them walked away.

"Nothing," grunted Peter.

"Peter," said Jordan gently.

"It's nothing, all right?" Peter snapped. "They're just – I used to be really good mates with those guys, back when we were the only kids our age in Phoenix."

"And now…?" Jordan prodded.

"And now I'm not," he said bitterly. "A month ago, when the really big rush of people came into Phoenix, those guys suddenly started cutting me out of their lives. Shutting down conversations as soon as I came near them, slipping off after school and not telling me where they were going…"

Jordan stared at him. "You don't think they have something to do with –?"

"Calvin?" Peter snorted. "Yeah, right. Those three couldn't keep something like that quiet if their lives depended on it."

Jordan shrugged. "Well, you know them better than I do. But I'm starting to think we're too far down the rabbit hole to rule anything –"

"Whoa," said Peter, closing his laptop suddenly.

"Whoa, what?" I said, looking around.

"Rabbit hole," said Peter, which wasn't exactly helpful. He stood up and slung his bag over his shoulder. "Library," he said. "C'mon!"

"Huh?" said Jordan. "Peter, what are you talking about?"

But he was already halfway across the playground.

Jordan and I grabbed our bags and chased after him.

The bell went as we reached the building, and kids started pouring into the stairwell between us and Peter. By the time we caught up with him, he was already halfway through the library door.

The library was empty except for a couple of Year 12 kids studying at the back. Peter glanced at the checkout desk, saw that no one was there, then shrugged and raced across to the fiction section.

"Carroll, right?" he said, running his finger along a row of books. Every single book looked unread.

"What are you doing?" I said, surprised that Peter even knew his way around a bookshelf.

"Never mind, found it." Peter pulled a paperback from the shelf and waved it in front of us.

Alice's Adventures in Wonderland

"Is that supposed to mean something?" Jordan asked, glancing at me.

"It means I finally figured out where – oh hey, miss!"

Mrs. Lewis, the school librarian, had just appeared from around the corner, pushing a cart loaded with books. She was an older lady, somewhere between my mum and my grandma, with a wrinkled face and hair that looked like it had just crossed the line from mostly brown to mostly gray.

"Hello, Peter," she smiled. "Shouldn't you be on your way to your next lesson?"

"Free period," Peter lied.

Mrs. Lewis pursed her lips at him.

"Okay, fine," said Peter, "I'm supposed to be in health – but I just need to check something really quickly!"

"Go on then," she sighed. "But let no one say that I didn't *try* to get you to do the right thing!" She stuck a book from her cart back onto the shelf. "And don't come running to me if someone catches you skipping class."

Peter grinned. "No worries, miss."

"And don't forget you've still got *Utopia* out," she told him, shelving a couple more books. "It was due back last Friday."

"Can I have it for another week?" Peter asked, as though oblivious to the disbelieving looks that Jordan and I were shooting him. "I'm still reading it."

"Oh, I suppose so," she said, smiling at Peter like he was her favorite grandchild. She grabbed on to her cart again and disappeared down the next row of shelves.

"Thanks, miss!" Peter called after her.

He turned back and caught me smirking at him. *"What?"*

"Bit old for you, don't you think?" I whispered.

"What's that supposed to mean?" said Peter defensively.

"Nothing," I said, still grinning. "I just didn't realize you and the librarian had such a *connection.*"

"Shut up," said Peter, punching me in the arm. "She just likes me because I borrow a lot of books."

Jordan raised an eyebrow. "You?"

"What, you think I'm illiterate just because I don't like school?" said Peter. "For your information, I'm not *dumb*, I have an *attitude problem.*"

"Ah," said Jordan seriously. "Of course."

"Just ask Staples!" said Peter. "I'm sure she'd be happy to tell you how much wasted potential I have."

"So are you ready to explain why you dragged us here in the first place?" I asked.

Peter's eyes flashed back down to the book in his hand like he'd forgotten he was even holding it.

"Right!" he said excitedly, opening it up and flipping through the pages. "Yeah, okay, so you know all that stuff Crazy Bill was shouting out at the airport?" he whispered. "All that raving about the trial and all that?"

"What about it?" I asked.

"It wasn't just raving," said Peter, frantically turning pages. "I *knew* I'd heard it before and I finally figured out why. It's a poem, from this book, somewhere near the beginning, I –"

Peter froze, eyes glued to the open book. Then he slowly turned the book around and held the page up in front of our faces. Like he'd said, there was a poem there. The words were all arranged into the shape of a mouse's tail and I recognized some of them from Crazy Bill's dummy spit at the airport.

But it wasn't the poem that had stopped Peter in his tracks. A picture had been drawn across the page in black marker, over the top of the printed text.

It was kind of hard to figure out what we were looking at. There was a cluster of boxes, like a bird's eye view of a little town, with a line stretching out that might have been a road, and lots of messy scribbles that I guessed were probably trees. Then I noticed two big Xs, one on the road and one in the trees, and suddenly realized what I was seeing.

"A map," said Peter. "That crazy psycho left us a map."

Chapter 16

I sat on my bed, flicking through the 150 still-not-working satellite channels, waiting for Peter to show up.

We'd spent the rest of yesterday trying to make sense of Crazy Bill's map. It hadn't taken long to figure out that the little town was Phoenix, and that the two Xs were places along the main road out of town.

But after a whole afternoon of throwing around theories about what could be out there that Crazy Bill was trying to point us to, we'd eventually decided – much to Peter's disappointment – that the only way we were ever going to find out was by following the map and checking it out for ourselves.

Thanks to the curfew, there wasn't really much we could do until the weekend, but we'd decided to meet at Jordan's house after school to come up with some sort of plan. Jordan was already there, but her parents had asked her to come straight home from school for a family meeting or something, so Peter and I had both gone home to wait for a couple of hours before we went over.

For a while, I'd actually been trying to catch up on some homework. But when you know the human race is about to be wiped off the face of the earth, quadratic equations suddenly seem a whole new level of pointless.

At about ten to five, the doorbell rang. I grabbed my backpack and went downstairs.

But when I got to the door, it wasn't Peter. It was Mr. Ketterley, the guy who'd met Mum and me at the airport. It was strange to think that had only been a week ago.

"Hey there, Luke," he said. "Is your mother around?"

"No," I said slowly, wondering what this was

about. "She's still at work. Why?"

"Just doing my rounds," Mr. Ketterley smiled. "Thought I'd drop by to check that you two are settling in okay. What about you, buddy? Got everything you need?"

I could think of about a hundred different responses to that question, but I wasn't about to say any of them out loud.

"What's the story with the phones?" I asked, already knowing what the answer would be.

"Still working on it," said Mr. Ketterley. "We're having a tough time figuring out the exact source of the problem. But we'll get there, kiddo, don't you worry about that. I'll be sure to let you know as soon as we're back online."

"Thanks."

"You miss your dad, huh?" he said, looking genuinely sorry about it.

I shrugged. I'd been trying not to think about it too much. "I just don't like being so cut off, you know?"

"Why don't you write him a letter?" Mr. Ketterley suggested. "Stick it in the mailbox and they'll send it out with the next supply truck."

"Yeah," I said, catching sight of Peter wheeling his bike in through the gate. "Yeah, okay, I'll do that."

"G'day, Aaron," said Peter, coming up the walkway, looking slightly confused to see him there.

"Oh hey, Pete," said Mr. Ketterley. "You two off somewhere?"

"Friend's place," said Peter.

"Right." Mr. Ketterley smiled again. "I'd better be on my way, then. Let your mother know I came by, will you, Luke?"

"Sure."

"And make sure you two are home by the time it gets dark," he said, looking up at the sky. A strange look flashed across his face. "You wouldn't want Officer Calvin to catch you breaking his new curfew."

"So, you're still not buying any of this?" I said as we rode past the Shackleton Building and out behind the school a few minutes later. "Even after the map?"

"The map proves nothing, mate," said Peter. "If I got into your math textbook and wrote you a letter saying the saucer people were invading, would you believe that too?"

"What do you think is out there then?" I asked. "I mean, he's obviously got *something* to show us."

"How should I know?" said Peter. "Maybe Crazy Bill's got a shack out there in the bush or something. Turn right up here," he added, pointing to a side street up ahead.

"A shack?" I smirked as we rounded the corner. "And he's, what, inviting us over for dinner?"

"All right, genius, what do *you* reckon is out there?"

"Dunno," I admitted. "Don't think he's trying to organize another meeting, though. At least, that's not all he's doing. There are two places marked, right? I reckon there's stuff out there that he wants us to see."

"Oh, good," said Peter. "So you've narrowed it down to *something*."

"Two somethings," I corrected.

"Right, well, that's *much* better." He pointed up ahead again. "It's on the end here. The one with the swing set."

"Uh-huh," I said. "Do I want to know how you know *exactly* where Jordan's house is?"

"Probably not," he grinned.

"You know, I think you may have actually crossed the line into stalker territory."

"Nah," said Peter. "It's only stalking if you get obsessive about it."

The whole town of Phoenix was pretty much just one big ring of houses with the town center in the middle. Jordan lived at the far end of her street, which meant that her house pressed right up against the bushland on one side, with only a bike path and about fifty meters of grass separating her place from the trees.

We pulled up at the house and dropped our bikes on the front lawn.

"What I don't understand," I said as we walked up the front walkway, "is why Bill thought shouting out some random poem was a good way of leading us to his map. What made him think we'd ever figure out that his jabbering was something from a book?"

"Probably just the first thing that popped into his head," Peter said with a shrug. "I mean, he didn't exactly have a lot of thinking time, did he?"

"So you don't reckon he drew that map until *after* the airport?"

"Why would he?" said Peter. "If security hadn't

152

come and broken up our meeting, he could've just shown us this stuff himself, right?"

"But then how'd he get into the library without being seen?" I asked, reaching for the doorbell.

Peter didn't have an answer to that one.

We heard the sound of running footsteps inside and then a girl, maybe five or six years old, opened the door. She was like a half-size scale model of Jordan, exactly the same, right down to the Phoenix school uniform and the braids in her hair.

"Who are you?" she asked, gazing up at us.

"We're here to see Jordan," Peter said.

The little girl's eyes went wide and a huge smile spread across her face. "Are you her *boyfriends?*" she gasped.

"No," I said quickly, "we're just —"

"You *are!*" she said. "I know you are!" She ran away down the hall, giggling, "Jordan! Jordan! Your boyfriends are here to see you! They want to give you a kiss!"

Peter shrugged. I raised an eyebrow at him and walked inside.

This was the first time since arriving in Phoenix

that I'd been inside anyone else's house, and it was a really weird experience. It was like walking into my own home after school one day and discovering that another family had moved in and replaced me. Jordan's house was *exactly* the same as mine – same rooms, same furniture, same everything.

Mini-Jordan reappeared in the hall, still giggling, dragging the real Jordan by the arm.

"Come on!" she said, pulling Jordan down the hall with both hands. "See? Here they are! Now, which one are you going to marry?"

Jordan sighed and said, "I see you've met my sister." There was a weird look on her face. A sort of shellshocked expression.

Jordan's little sister was staring back up at Peter and me now. Her face was twisted in concentration, like she was sizing the two of us up.

"You should marry that one," she said suddenly, pointing at me. "He's the handsomest one."

"You've *gotta* be kidding me," said Peter with mock indignation.

"Come on, Georgia," said a voice from the family room. "Let's give Jordan and her friends a bit of space."

A woman who had to be Jordan's mum stepped out into the hall and gave the little girl a stern look. She had the same worn-out expression on her face that Jordan did, and looked like she might have been crying.

"Oh Mum, can't I play with them?" Mini-Jordan pleaded.

"No, Georgia."

Georgia balled up her fists and let out an angry groan. She stomped her foot and stormed off into the family room.

Jordan smiled wearily at her mum. "Thanks."

A second later, a huge guy with a shaved head appeared in the doorway. Jordan's dad, I assumed. He looked like he'd just gotten home from work; his collar was open and a half-undone tie was still hanging from his neck. He put an arm around his wife's waist and looked down at Peter and me.

"This is Luke and Peter," said Jordan, waving a hand at the two of us.

"Right," I said. "I mean, hi."

If there's a not-slightly-awkward way to meet your friend's parents, I'd love to know about it.

For a minute, Jordan's dad just kept on staring down at us. Then his face broke into a grin. He stretched out an enormous hand and said, "Nice to meet you both."

"Y-yeah," said Peter. "You too."

Jordan's dad glanced back towards the family room as he heard Georgia yelling for him. He called out, "Coming, sweetheart!" and went off to find her.

"Make sure you don't forget your homework, Jordan," her mum said over her shoulder as she followed Jordan's dad back into the family room.

"*Okay*, Mum," said Jordan, rolling her eyes and turning back to Peter and me. "C'mon, let's go to my room."

"Is everything okay?" I asked as we went down the hall. "You look –"

"Yeah, fine," said Jordan unconvincingly.

"Wait. Did you tell your family about –?"

"About Tabitha?" said Jordan, lowering her voice slightly. "No, of course not."

Jordan's bedroom turned out to be downstairs, in what we were using as a spare room at my place. The furniture was all laid out exactly the same as my room – desk in the corner, flat-screen TV mounted on the wall, walk-in closet, big double bed with identical blue-and-white sheets – and again, I got that weird déjà vu feeling as I walked in.

Jordan shut the door behind us and sat down on the edge of her bed. She stared at the carpet, resting her elbows on her knees, and let out a sigh.

"It's Mum," she said, without looking up. "You know those doctor's appointments? She's just found out she's –"

"She's sick, isn't she?" Peter finished. He sat down next to Jordan and moved to put an arm around her. "Jordan, that's –"

"No, you idiot," said Jordan, shrugging him off. "She's pregnant."

Chapter 17

"Pregnant?" I repeated. "Isn't that…? That's good news, right?"

"Is it?" said Jordan heavily. "A new baby, here in this town? With everything that's going on?"

"But still," I said, trying to be encouraging, "a new brother or sister…"

"Yeah," she nodded, standing up. "And there's part of me that…" She sighed again and threw up her hands. "I don't know."

"What about your mum, though?" Peter asked, obviously trying to recover from Jordan's brush-off. "How come she's so upset? Like, I get that you're worried about all this apocalypse stuff, but she doesn't know anything about that."

"She's not stupid, Peter," Jordan snapped. "She might not know everything we know, but it doesn't take a genius to figure out that things in Phoenix aren't exactly normal."

"Sure, but –" Peter tried again.

"She doesn't even want to be here! She only agreed to come because Dad got laid off back in Brisbane and then both of them magically got offered these great jobs in Phoenix, and so we fly all the way out here and suddenly we're cut off from everything and we can't even call back home –" She glared at Peter as he opened his mouth again, "– and I swear, Weir, if you try to tell me one more time that none of this is real, I'm going to smack your little –"

"Okay, fine, but –"

"But *what?*" she demanded.

Peter shrank back against the bed.

Jordan turned away from him and went over to the other side of the room. She leaned back against the wall and sank down to the carpet, worn out from the effort of getting that off her chest. It was like this news about the baby had shaken some part of her that none of the rest of it had been able to touch. She had a look on her face like she didn't know whether she wanted to cry or punch someone.

I went over and sat down opposite her, a bit out of arm's reach just in case. "Jordan," I said, with no idea how I was going to finish the sentence. "It's not going to happen. This whole end-of-the-world thing, we can't – we won't let it happen. We're going to do something about it."

Of course, I realized immediately how *ridiculous* that sounded.

But Jordan looked at me and nodded. Not like she believed me, but I think she at least appreciated the attempt to make her feel better. She closed her eyes for a minute, then took a breath and said, "I just keep thinking about – by the time this baby is born, Mum's only a couple of months pregnant, she won't even give birth until after…" She trailed off.

Across the room, I saw Peter sitting up. He stared down at us, like he was itching to say something, but he didn't open his mouth.

I glanced back over at Jordan, but I still didn't

have any answers for her. The whole thing was just too big. Coded messages and secret conspiracies and superpowered homeless people.

"Maybe it's time to tell someone else what's going on here," I said after a while. "I mean, the end of the world? I think it's safe to say we're in over our heads."

"Who are we going to tell?" said Jordan. "Anything we say to security is going to get straight back to Calvin. And Ms. Pryor's in his pocket too, so we can't tell anyone at school. And who knows who else is in on it?"

"Then our families, at least," I suggested. "I mean, if you tell your parents what's going on –"

"No," said Jordan firmly, before I could even finish my sentence. "They'd – if my parents found out, they'd want to rush straight out there and take Calvin on themselves."

"Isn't that what you want?" said Peter. "People to help –"

"Not them. I'm not putting my family in danger. If Calvin gets it in his head that they might expose him … I'm not letting that happen."

She was right. My mum might not be about to

get into a fight with Calvin, but she wasn't exactly subtle. It'd be only a matter of time before she lost her temper and let something slip. Right now, the safest thing we could do for our families was make sure they didn't know anything about this.

"So . . . what?" I said helplessly. "What do we do?"

Jordan sat up, a flicker of her usual determination back in her eyes. "We need to get out," she said. "Get across to the next town and warn someone *outside* about what's going on."

"How are we going to do that?" I said. "I mean, with the airport shut down and everything."

"There's still the main road out of town."

"Yeah, and no cars. How far do you think we're going to get on bikes?"

"Why don't we find out?" said Jordan. "We need to go out there anyway if we're going to follow Crazy Bill's map, right? So why don't we go for a ride on the weekend and see what we can figure out?"

"All right," I said, shrugging. "Yeah. I mean, it's the closest thing we've got to a —"

"Do you guys really want to do that?" Peter cut in. "You really want to go chasing after Crazy Bill again? You want to risk winding up like those security guys back at the airport?"

"Oh, so you *do* think he's dangerous?" said Jordan, her head jerking up to glare at him.

"Never said he wasn't," said Peter, flinching slightly. "I still don't reckon he's got superpowers or whatever, but you've only got to take one look at those guards in the medical center to see that he –"

"You know what, Peter?" Jordan spat. "No one's asking you to come with us."

From the look on Peter's face, she might as well have punched him.

"I – I know that," he said. "But I don't want *you* to get yourself killed either. I know you guys still reckon this is all real, but think about it – what are you actually basing that on?"

And suddenly it was my turn to get angry.

"Listen," I hissed, something snapping inside my head, "my dad is out there, all right? And according to Calvin, he's got ninety-two days left to live. So maybe you can afford to waste time messing around and acting like none of this is actually happening, but I can't, okay? I can't."

Peter was shaking his head. "Mate, I wasn't –"

"You don't want it to be true," I said over the top of him. "I get that. I'm not exactly thrilled about it myself. But it's happening. So you need to decide whether you're with us or not. Or else you might wind up with a couple more friends who don't have time for you anymore."

It wasn't meant to be a threat. Not really. But we didn't have time to waste sitting around waiting for Peter to decide whose team he was on.

Peter looked at me, then over at Jordan. He stared at her for a long time, like he was trying to decide whether she was worth all this effort. "All right," he said finally, closing his eyes like he was trying to wish it all away. "Yeah, all right. I'm in."

"Okay." I nodded, dropping down into Jordan's desk chair. "Right. Good. That's good."

You know those conversations that are so full-on, you actually come away feeling physically exhausted? Turns out deciding what to do about the end of the world can really take it out of you.

I swiveled the chair around to face Jordan. "All right. So, Saturday. What are we –?"

But Jordan wasn't listening. She was on her feet, staring across the room. Her eyes were locked on her bedroom window.

Standing outside, face pressed up against the glass, tears streaming down his face, was Crazy Bill.

Chapter 18

WEDNESDAY, MAY 13
92 DAYS

Before I even had time to register what was going on,
Jordan had dropped down and grabbed a hockey stick
from under her bed. She ran over, threw the window
open and took a swing at Crazy Bill's head.

"No, *please*," he said, staggering out of the way,
eyes red from crying.

"WHAT?" Jordan shouted. "WHAT DO YOU
WANT?" She leaned out the window and jabbed the
hockey stick at him like a spear.

"Jordan, be careful!" said Peter as he and I sprang
to our feet.

"GET – AWAY – FROM – MY – HOUSE!"

Jordan yelled, emphasizing each word with another swing of the stick.

"I wasn't –" Crazy Bill sobbed, tears turning to mud on his filthy cheeks. "I only wanted to –"

Jordan's bedroom door flew open behind us, and her dad burst into the room. Crazy Bill took one look at him and bolted. Not that I could blame him. Jordan was scary enough, but her dad looked like he could drive him into the ground with one punch.

Then again, Crazy Bill wasn't exactly defenseless.

Jordan pulled her head back inside, breathing hard. Her dad barreled past her, vaulted out through the window, and took off after Crazy Bill.

"Dad, no!" Jordan yelled. "He'll –"

But he was already halfway down the street.

Guess that's where Jordan gets her reckless streak, I thought.

"We need to follow them!" she said urgently, pulling herself up onto the window frame.

I spun around at the sound of footsteps. Jordan's mum came racing into the room with Georgia on her heels. Jordan stopped, halfway out the window.

"What are you *doing?*" her mum gasped.

"Crazy Bill!" said Jordan, eyes flitting wildly between her mum and the street outside. "The homeless man! Dad went after him. I need to go and –"

"No," said her mum. "Get back inside. Let your father –"

"No – Mum – you don't –"

Georgia ran to look out the window, but her mum grabbed onto her. "Stay here, sweetheart." She turned back to Jordan. "Are you all right? Did he hurt you?"

"I'm fine," Jordan muttered, still perched on the windowsill. But there was panic all over her face and I knew exactly what she was thinking.

If Crazy Bill freaked out again…

I stared out the window, heart thumping, but there was no sign of either her dad or Crazy Bill.

Surely he wouldn't do anything. Not in the middle of town. Not when –

"Mum, listen," Jordan pleaded. "We need to go out there and –"

"*No,* Jordan."

Georgia started to cry, probably more confused than anything else, but clearly realizing that something was wrong. Her mum bent down to pick her up.

"What did he want?" she asked Jordan. "Did he say anything to you?"

"No, he was just staring at us." Jordan stuck her foot back out the window.

"Jordan!" warned her mum. "Don't you dare –"

"Mrs. Burke –" Peter began.

Georgia was almost screaming now. Patting her on the back with one hand, Jordan's mum crossed the room to pull Jordan away from the window with the other.

"Mum – *stop* –" Jordan wrenched her way free. "You don't understand –"

"Jordan, that man is *dangerous*. You can't –"

"Mrs. Burke," Peter tried again, "we –"

"All of you need to calm down and – *Jordan!* I told you to *stop!*"

Jordan was back at the window. She leaned out again, then reeled back as a face appeared in front of her.

It was her dad, sweating through his work shirt, chest heaving.

For a second, no one moved. Then Jordan launched herself at her dad and gave him a hug.

"Hey, come on," he said, putting an arm around her. "Jordan, I'm fine! Take it easy."

She released him and he leaned against the windowsill for support.

"Did you get him?" Jordan's mum asked.

"Almost had him," he panted. "Chased him down to the end of the street, but he got away into the park. You all okay?" he asked, glancing at Jordan.

She nodded silently, and my thoughts flashed painfully back to my own dad.

"That park's always crawling with security," Jordan's mum said. "Surely one of them will have spotted him running through."

"Maybe," said Jordan's dad, sweat still dripping down from his shaven head, "but I'm going to ride down to the security center anyway. Let them know we saw him."

"Okay, good idea," said Jordan's mum, switching a still-whimpering Georgia across into her other arm.

"Keep the doors and windows locked until I get home," Jordan's dad said, "just in case he comes back." He wiped his brow with the back of his hand. "Right, back soon."

He disappeared, and Jordan's mum pulled the window closed behind him. She flipped the lock, then turned back to Peter and me, and said, "You boys had better get moving too. It's almost dark out there."

"Okay, yeah," I said. "Well…thanks for having us."

She gave us a wry smile. "I just want to let you know this is not a typical Wednesday night at our house," she said. "Things around here are normally much more…normal."

"No worries, Mrs. Burke," said Peter. "I've pretty much given up on normal anyway."

THURSDAY, MAY 14
91 DAYS

My alarm went off earlier than usual the next morning.

There'd been an email from Jordan waiting for me when I'd gotten home the night before, asking me to meet her in the town center before school.

She hadn't said what it was about, so as I rode up the street towards the fountain, my mind raced with a hundred ugly possibilities. Had Crazy Bill come back to her place after we'd left? Had her dad been attacked on his way to the security center? Had Jordan found some new bit of information about what Calvin was up to?

I met Jordan outside the bakery. She shoved a paper bag and a coffee cup into my hand and sat down on a bench next to one of the gardens running along the street.

"Thanks," I said, sitting down next to her. "Is everything okay?"

"Yeah, no, nothing's happened," she said, taking a sip from her cup. "I just – I don't know. I guess I just wanted to talk to you about everything that's happened... Away from Peter, you know?"

"Oh," I said blankly. I knew Peter had been annoying her, but...

"Not that I don't – you know," she said hurriedly. "But he's kind of –"

"No, I get it," I said, pulling a croissant out of the paper bag. "So, was everything okay at your place last night, after we left?"

"Yeah, Crazy Bill didn't come back. Dad put in a report at the security center, but he didn't really tell them anything they didn't already know."

"Bill would've been long gone by then anyway," I said.

"Mmm," she said, taking another sip of her hot chocolate. "Hey, listen, sorry about yesterday."

"What about it?" I said through a mouthful of croissant.

"You know, me freaking out over the baby and stuff."

"Jordan, you're *allowed* to freak out," I said, swallowing. "In the same week, you've found out that the whole world is about to be blown to bits *and* that your mum's going to have another kid. I reckon that's a pretty normal reaction."

"Yeah, but it's not me," said Jordan with a sigh. "I don't usually get, you know, *scared* like that. I'm stronger than that."

"Oh," I said stupidly. "I mean, yes, of course you are. But that doesn't mean – look, you don't have to be strong *all* the time."

You don't have to be strong all the time? Brilliant. Great comforting, idiot.

Jordan didn't say anything. She just gazed off in the other direction.

I ripped another piece off the croissant and stuck it in my mouth.

My eyes drifted across to the security center, and I saw Officer Reeve walking down the steps. He was still bound up in plaster and bandages, but he was back in his security uniform again. Back on patrol.

A little shuddering noise to my left brought my attention back to Jordan. She had turned back to face me again. Her mouth was doing this weird creasing thing, like she was trying to smile and frown at the same time. And she was *crying*.

I'd made her cry.

Or, no, *something* had made her cry. It might not have been me. I don't know.

Forget the end of the world, there's nothing scarier or more confusing than a crying girl.

For a minute, it was like I was stunned. I just sat there looking at her, watching the tears streaming down her face. Then I stretched out my arm and put it around her and pulled her into a hug. Because that's what you do, right?

She put her head down on my shoulder and her braids all fell in my face.

We sat there like that for a minute, with me desperately trying to come up with something reassuring to say.

Then she lifted her head, sat back up again, and said, "Sorry."

"What?" I said. "No, don't – it's okay."

"Usually my family are the ones I –"

She stopped.

I heard running footsteps. An animal scream.

Then a shoulder collided with my face and suddenly I was on the ground.

Chapter 19

THURSDAY, MAY 14
91 DAYS

For the first few seconds, I had no idea what was going on.

My head slammed back against the low brick wall of the garden behind me. The whole world exploded and turned red. I closed my eyes and shouted, but no sound came out. Then a heavy weight came crashing down on my chest, pinning me to the ground. I saw matted hair and two bulging eyes, only inches from mine.

It was Crazy Bill.

He let out a scream that was more like a growl. Spit sprayed across my face. Between the smell and the concussion, I almost gagged.

My eyes refocused just long enough to catch sight of Jordan lying on the other side of the bench. She'd dived out of the way just in time. I stretched out a hand, dizzy, disoriented. Jordan staggered to her feet.

Crazy Bill sat up, his body still crushing my legs, and screamed again.

For a second, Jordan was on his back, trying to shove him aside. But then Bill twisted around and threw back his shoulder and she was gone. There was a muffled thud as Jordan landed. I looked up, trying to see what had happened to her, but a fist to my gut brought me straight back down to the ground, blasting the air out of my lungs.

"NO!" Crazy Bill shouted. "YOU HAVE TO – I *NEED* – AARGH!"

He threw down another fist. I tried to get out of the way, but my head was still spinning. Searing pain shot through my side as his fist landed just below my rib cage.

"Stop," I groaned thickly. "Bill, please –?"

"YOU – YOU DON'T –" he raged, his whole body trembling, "I ALREADY – *KILLED –!*"

He grabbed me by the shirt and started shaking me violently against the concrete, wrenching my shoulders. I vaguely noticed a crowd beginning to gather, blurry figures in a circle all around us, but so far no one seemed that keen on stepping in to help me.

"Quick!" Jordan was shouting. "Why isn't anybody – somebody help him!"

So she was okay. Or at least –

Another fist, like fire tearing its way through my face. Crazy Bill had given up trying to form actual words and was now just letting out furious growls with each blow.

"Please!" someone screamed. "Calvin! Where's Officer Calvin?"

"No –" I spluttered, blood bubbling out of my mouth. My head hit the bricks again and this time I was sure it was splitting right open. I felt my eyes start to roll back into my head.

"He's coming," said another voice. "He's running back with the …"

I woke up with the mother of all headaches and a bright white light shining down on my face.

"Where am I?" I croaked.

I pushed down against the mattress beneath me, trying to sit up. Pain ripped through my head and I collapsed back onto the bed, gasping.

"Easy there," said a calm voice from somewhere nearby.

I blinked my eyes, squinting at the harsh whiteness around me, and the room slowly came into focus.

I was lying in a hospital bed. A man with a beard was smiling down at me.

"No sudden movements, Luke," he said. "You took quite a beating back there."

There was a mechanical whirring noise as the doctor adjusted the bed, shifting me up into something closer to a sitting position. From here, I could see three other beds, all of them empty.

"I'm Doctor Robert Montag," he said, bringing over a glass of water, "Head Physician here at Phoenix Medical."

He took two white tablets out of a plastic jar and handed them to me.

"What's this?" I asked. I suddenly realized how dry my throat was.

"Panadeine," said Dr. Montag. "For your head."

I swallowed the painkillers and handed the empty glass back to the doctor. "What about Jordan?" I said, remembering. "She was —"

"She's fine," said Dr. Montag reassuringly. "And so are you, all things considered. You were unconscious for less than half an hour. You've got a mild concussion, a split lip, and some impressive-looking bruises, but that's about the worst of it."

"And Crazy Bill?" I added, wincing.

"Sitting in a holding cell in the security center," said Dr. Montag. "Let me tell you, you're very fortunate to be in such good shape after a run-in with that man. Not everyone who's met him has come away with such minor injuries. I've got a security guard next door who's still fighting for his life."

The bed whirred again and in a few seconds I was lying down.

"You, on the other hand," said Dr. Montag, "should be out of here by this time tomorrow."

"Tomorrow?"

"I'd like to keep you here overnight, just to be on the safe side. Your parents have been informed, and they can –"

"*Parent*," I corrected.

"Sorry?"

"My parents are divorced. Dad doesn't live here."

Dr. Montag's smile flickered. "Oh. I'm sorry," he said.

The longer my eyes stayed open, the more I felt like throwing up. I closed them again and rolled over onto my side. I swallowed, trying to keep the bile down.

"You, uh, also have a couple of visitors waiting outside who'd like to see you for a few minutes, if you're feeling up to it," said Dr. Montag.

"Mmhmm," I said, already on the verge of sleep again.

But then I heard slow footsteps and the sound of a crutch tapping along on the floor. Officer Calvin was hobbling into the room. Ms. Pryor was right behind him. My stomach plummeted. *Now what?*

"Close the door on your way out, will you, Rob?" Calvin said.

"Hmm?" said Dr. Montag. "Oh. Yes, of course."

He disappeared from the room, pulling the door shut behind him.

Ms. Pryor pulled up a chair and sat down at my bedside in a not-very-convincing imitation of a concerned parent. "Hello, Luke," she said. "How are you feeling?"

"All right," I said, opening my eyes again and trying to keep my voice even.

"We'd like to ask you a few questions about what happened this morning, if we may," said Calvin, standing next to Ms. Pryor. There were plenty of other seats in the room, but he seemed to prefer towering over the top of me.

I guess he was trying to be intimidating. It was working.

"Why did Crazy Bill attack you this morning?" he asked.

"I don't know."

For once, playing dumb and being honest were pretty much the same thing.

"All right," said Calvin, clearly not buying it. "Why do you *think* he attacked you?"

"I don't know," I said again. "We were just talking."

182

"You were *talking* to him?" said Ms. Pryor. "After both Officer Calvin and I specifically warned –"

"No!" I said hurriedly. "No, I wasn't, I was talking to *Jordan*."

"Oh," said Ms. Pryor, leaning closer. "And what were you and Jordan talking about?"

"Nothing," I said. "I mean, nothing to make Crazy Bill want to attack me. I was just at her place last night, and we found out that her mum's having a –"

I stopped mid-sentence. I was sore and groggy and it was hard to keep straight in my head what was safe to tell them and what wasn't.

"– having a hard time settling in," I finished. "You know, moving away from her family and friends and everything. Jordan just wanted someone to talk to about it."

"I see," said Ms. Pryor slowly, eyebrows raised. "And then, for no reason, you were attacked?"

"I guess."

"Do you expect us to believe," said Calvin, looming over me, "that this incident is completely unrelated to your meeting at the airport last Sunday? That you just *happened* to be in the wrong place at the wrong time with the wrong person, *twice?"*

"I don't know," I groaned, closing my eyes, wishing they would both just disappear. "I don't know what he wants. Haven't you caught him now? Why don't you ask *him* why he attacked me?"

"I'm sure Officer Calvin intends to do exactly that," said Ms. Pryor, "but as you can no doubt appreciate, it's important for us to hear your side of the story as well."

"A crazy homeless man ran up and punched my face in for no reason," I said. "That's my side of the story."

Calvin looked like he was about to shout at me, but Ms. Pryor stopped him with a sideways glance.

"Luke," she said gently, "please understand that Officer Calvin and I are on your side in all of this. We want to bring your attacker to justice, but to do that, we need to have a complete and accurate picture of the events leading up to the attack. We need you to tell us everything you know."

"That *is* everything I know," I said firmly.

Calvin stared down his broken nose at me. "All right," he said, eventually. "I'll give you the rest of the week to think about it. I'll be in touch after I've spoken to Bill."

He turned and began making his way towards the door. Ms. Pryor rushed to open it for him.

"If you happen to recall any other information that might be of assistance –" she called over her shoulder.

"Yeah," I lied. "I'll let you know."

I didn't see Calvin or Pryor again for the rest of the day.

I slept away most of the morning and woke up feeling much more human. My face still ached from all the scrapes and bruises, but the headaches were fading and so was the urge to throw up every time I moved.

Jordan dropped in to see me after school, but between the security cameras on the walls and the steady stream of doctors and nurses, we didn't feel comfortable discussing any of the things we *really* wanted to talk about.

Peter came by soon afterwards. He asked how I

was doing, then quickly launched into a story about how he'd tried all day to ask Jordan about the baby and how her mum was feeling, but for some reason she hadn't wanted to talk to him about it. I tried to be as supportive as I could without moving my head.

It was almost dark by the time Mum arrived at the medical center. I heard her storming up the corridor, shouting at any nurse unlucky enough to get in her way. It turned out she hadn't gotten the message about me being there until five minutes after she finished work. So she'd run straight over and, as usual, began looking for someone to blame.

I could hear Dr. Montag trying to convince her that it probably wasn't necessary to sue anyone over this, and she finally came in to see me. She asked most of the same questions that Calvin and Ms. Pryor had, but at least she believed me when I said I had no idea why I'd been attacked.

Mum disappeared for a while, then came back in with a change of clothes and a toothbrush and stuff for me.

"Let's go out for dinner tomorrow night," she

said, laying the clothes out on the chair next to my bed. "I feel like I've hardly seen you this week."

Yeah, whose fault is that? I thought bitterly. But I shoved the thought aside. "Sounds good," I said.

"Great," said Mum. "Where would you like to go?"

"You pick." To be honest, after a week and a half of macaroni and pizza, I would much rather have stayed at home and eaten something out of our own oven. But at least she was making the effort to do something together.

"How about one of those cafés out near the park?" she suggested. "I hear Cusumano's does great pasta."

"Sure."

Mum finished laying out my stuff and then kissed me goodbye. She switched the light off on her way out the door, throwing the big empty hospital room into shadow.

I rolled over to face the window and felt a flicker of panic as I saw something move past outside.

Just a bird.

I reminded myself that there was no one out there, that Crazy Bill was locked up in the security center, that his stalking days were over, at least for now. And I realized pretty quickly that this thought didn't make sleep come any easier.

Chapter 20

"Okay, here's the plan," said Jordan, unfolding a giant map and laying it out on my bed. "We take –"

"So we're definitely still going?" Peter interrupted. "Even though Crazy Bill's out of action? Even though we still have no idea what we're looking for and the only person who ever did is now sitting in prison?"

"Yep," said Jordan firmly.

"Right, just checking."

We were sitting in my bedroom, going over the plan that Jordan and Peter had come up with for investigating Crazy Bill's map.

I'd been released from the medical center in time

for school that morning, but Dr. Montag had sent me home, dosed up on painkillers, insisting that I stay there and rest. I wasn't about to turn down a long weekend, especially since this particular weekend was shaping up to be anything but relaxing.

So I'd emailed Jordan and Peter and got them to come around after school to bring me up to speed.

"This is a map of all the bike tracks and walking paths around Phoenix," Jordan said, smoothing out the big sheet of paper. "Seeing as Calvin's already got his eye on us, it probably wouldn't be such a smart idea to ride out onto the main road in front of everyone, so we're thinking we'll make our start here instead."

She pointed to a place on the map at the south end of town, where a narrow path stretched into the bush.

"This track goes straight into the bush for a kilometer or so," she said, tracing along the path with her finger, "then it curves around in a big circle and comes out near my house. But right here –" she ran her finger back along the line, "– the track runs right up against the main road, only a hundred meters away from it."

"So we ride out there and then cut through the

190

bush?" I asked, peering over her shoulder.

"Right," said Jordan. "That should get us far enough away from town to make sure no one sees us leaving. We'll have to make sure we don't run into any supply trucks coming down the road, but apart from that we should be safe."

"Until we get to whatever death trap Crazy Bill's got waiting for us out there," I muttered.

Not that I didn't still want to go ahead with our plan, but the pummeling I'd been given the day before had driven home for me just how dangerous this could get.

Jordan looked across the bed at me, concern flashing across her face. "Luke, if you want to leave this," she said, glancing at my battered face, "put it off for another week until you've recovered from –"

"No, I'm fine," I said, trying not to wince. My face hurt more when I was reminded of it. "It has to be tomorrow. We're already down to, what, ninety days? Something tells me we can't afford to lose another week. I'm just saying we're probably not going to like what we find out there."

Jordan was still staring at me. "I don't get it,"

she said. "One minute, Crazy Bill is feeding us information, and the next he's stalking us and beating us up. I wish he'd make up his mind about whose side he's on."

"I think Crazy Bill is on Crazy Bill's side," said Peter, leaning back in my desk chair. "I don't reckon he's done anything so far that wasn't helping *his* agenda."

"Maybe," I said, "but his map is still the only thing we have to go on right now."

"Great," said Peter. "When do we leave?"

Jordan picked up *Alice's Adventures in Wonderland* from the bed and flipped to Crazy Bill's map.

"Well," she said, "I'm assuming this thing isn't to scale, so it's hard to tell how far away either of these places actually are. But if we head off at, say, midday tomorrow, that gives us seven hours of riding time before the curfew kicks in, which is probably about as much as any of us can ride in a day anyway."

And that was pretty much as far as our planning went. Leave at noon. Cut through the bush. Ride down the road and see what happens. Genius.

We hung around in my room for a couple of

hours, playing video games and pretending that our lives were back to normal, until 5:30 p.m., when against all odds Mum came home from work in time for dinner.

Peter offered to walk Jordan home, which was ironic since I was sure she could have taken him down with one hand tied behind her back. To no one's surprise, she turned him down.

It was getting kind of depressing to see Peter crash and burn with every attempt to win Jordan over – like watching the same car crash replayed again and again in slow motion. But convincing him not to climb behind the wheel again was clearly a lost cause.

The others headed home, and Mum and I walked down the street to Cusumano's. We took a shortcut through the park, past families standing around barbecues, teenagers skateboarding and rollerblading, kids feeding ducks or getting pushed on the swings by their parents.

Normal people doing normal stuff.

After everything that had happened in the last week and a bit, it was weird to think that most people saw Phoenix as just a perfect little town.

I mean, sure, that scary homeless man would've given a few of them a fright, but that was taken care of now, and they could all go back to walking their dogs and planting their vegetable gardens.

Even Mum was still positive about the move to Phoenix. "I feel like things are starting to settle down for us now, don't you?" she said as we reached the café and found a table overlooking the playground.

I stared at her. "Mum, I just got hospitalized by a psychotic hobo. How is that settling down?"

She bit her lip. "Okay, point taken," she said, picking up a menu from the center of the table. "And I can hardly imagine how scary it must have been for you, being attacked out of nowhere like that by someone you've never even met."

"But…?"

"*But*," she continued, "that was just a freak accident. One in a million. You were just in the wrong place at the wrong time."

"Didn't feel very accidental when he was beating the crap out of me," I said.

A waitress, only a year or so older than me, appeared at our table. I thought maybe I recognized her from school. Her eyes went wide for a second at the sight of my bruised face, but she quickly covered up her shock and asked if we were ready to order.

"The point I'm trying to make," said Mum, after the waitress had disappeared into the kitchen again, "is that apart from that *one* incident, our move to Phoenix seems to be working out for the best."

"What about the phones?" I said skeptically. "I haven't talked to Dad since we left. For all he knows, our chopper disappeared into a black hole on the way here."

"Luke, if your father can't –" she paused midstream to rephrase what she'd been about to say. She'd been doing that a lot ever since Dad stopped being *Dad* and started being *your father*. "Look, I know you miss him, but I'm sure he understands that these things happen from time to time. It's just the nature of living in a small town."

"Uh-huh."

"Tell you what," Mum said. "First thing on Monday, I'll get in touch with Mr. Ketterley and pin down a date for your first flight back to Sydney."

Yeah, good luck with that. "Thanks," I said.

195

The food arrived a few minutes later, and it turned out to be pretty good. Better than most of the junk I'd been eating lately, anyway.

We talked about school and work and what Mum wanted to do with the backyard if she ever had time. I told her that I was going bike riding with Peter and Jordan tomorrow, and she said how great it was that I was making friends already.

But by the time we'd finished eating, the conversation had circled back around to Mum trying to reassure me – and probably herself as well – that moving to Phoenix had been the right choice.

"I know it's been a rocky start, Luke, but we're getting there. You can see that, right? I'm finally getting my head around this new job, you've got your new friends at school…"

She took my hand and held it between both of hers. "This town is a good place," she smiled. "Better for us than the big city. We just need to give ourselves enough time to find our feet. There's something different about Phoenix. The people in charge here – I get the feeling they really *believe* in something, don't you?"

I didn't answer.

I looked back out at the park, where a couple of security guys were coming around to enforce the curfew, which, I realized with a nasty jolt, hadn't been lifted even after Crazy Bill's capture. Armed men moving in to protect the secrets of Calvin and his friends.

Whatever it was that these people believed in, I could think of about seven billion others who might see things differently.

Chapter 21

Jordan arrived at my place at 11:30 the next morning, carrying her school bag over her shoulder. She opened it up on the coffee table, dumping out a bike pump, a pocket knife, a water bottle, a box of matches, a coil of rope, a notepad and pen, the bike track map from yesterday, some sandwiches, and a flashlight.

"You really think we're going to need all that?" I asked, popping some more painkillers into my mouth as she piled everything back into the bag.

"Doubt it," she shrugged, closing the bag again. "But we might need some of it."

Peter showed up about forty-five minutes later,

looking like he'd just rolled out of bed.

In another surprising display of motherly kindness (maybe she really *was* starting to make an effort), Mum offered to make lunch for us before we left.

"Thanks, Mrs. Hunter," said Peter. "That would be –"

"We really should be going," said Jordan pointedly. "Thank you, though."

Peter sighed.

"Oh, stop whingeing," Jordan muttered as we walked our bikes out into the street. "There's food in my bag if you're hungry. Have you got the map?"

"Right here," said Peter, patting the back pocket of his jeans and putting on his best non-whingeing face.

It only took us about a minute to ride out to the edge of town. At the end of my street were about ten different bike paths and walking trails leading off into the bush. They branched off from a wooden information stand with safety advice and litter warnings and a blown-up version of the map Jordan had been using yesterday. There were other people gathered around the map, figuring out which path they wanted to take.

"See, this is what people are reduced to when

there's no TV," Peter explained.

Jordan studied the big map for a minute, then pointed at one of the dirt tracks and said, "That one. Let's go."

The track turned out to be a lot rougher and bumpier than the one out to the airport, and a couple of times I almost stacked my bike over a rock or a fallen tree branch. Even so, I had to admit that it was peaceful out here, riding along and watching the scenery go by. Or at least it would've been for someone with normal-sized problems to worry about.

"How do we know when it's time to turn off?" I asked.

"There should be a rock formation coming up on the left," said Jordan, looking up the road. "Like a great big boulder with another couple of – look, there it is!"

We stopped at Jordan's pile of rocks and waited a few minutes until we were sure no one else was coming past. A few other cyclists zoomed past us – full-on bike freaks with streamlined helmets, riding goggles, and skintight bodysuits that left way too little to the imagination.

We must have looked kind of suspicious waiting there by the side of the path because one of them pulled to a stop next to us. He took off his helmet, revealing a familiar orange comb-over.

"Mr. Hanger?" said Jordan, raising an eyebrow.

Mr. Hanger shot us all a dangerous look. "What are you three doing out here?" he demanded.

Some teachers just never know when to stop being teachers.

"We're riding our bikes, sir," said Peter. "What does it look like?"

"Peter, I don't appreciate –"

"Sir, it's Saturday," Peter said. "You're supposed to be off duty. Give us a break, will you?"

Mr. Hanger snarled. He looked like he was dying to find some way to ruin our day, but I guess he realized there wasn't much he could do to us on the weekend, so he just gritted his teeth and ordered us to stay out of trouble.

"You should go home and read my new essay, sir," said Peter as Mr. Hanger prepared to leave. "It's a real page-turner."

"I'll thank you not to tell me how to spend my

weekend," barked Mr. Hanger, putting his helmet back on. "For your information, those papers have already been marked – *even* those that had to be resubmitted."

"Pretty good stuff, huh, sir?" said Peter.

"Yes, much better," grumbled Mr. Hanger, swinging a leg up over his bike and pushing off down the path again.

"Idiot," Peter muttered.

We waited until he was fifty meters down the road, and then we slipped away into the trees.

Unfortunately, cutting across through the bush to the main road was not as easy as we expected. It would've been fine if it was just us on foot, but try dragging three bikes through a hundred meters of rocks and branches and fallen trees.

"You know what?" said Peter as we finally scrambled out by the side of the main road. "I'm suddenly feeling a whole lot better about this trip."

"Why's that?" I asked him.

"I just survived seeing Mr. Hanger in spandex," he said. "Whatever Crazy Bill wants to show us out here, there's no way it's gonna be scarier than –"

"Truck!" said Jordan. "Quick, get down."

We crouched behind a bush at the edge of the road as the truck sped past, carrying supplies into town.

"Should be okay for a while now," said Peter as we stood up again. "There's usually only a couple of trucks a day, tops."

After almost two weeks of getting around on Phoenix's narrow, gray bike paths, it was weird being back on a real road again. We stuck close to the edge as we rode along, ready to dive back into the bushes if we needed to.

At first, I was constantly craning my neck around, eyes peeled for anything out of the ordinary. But after an hour or more of riding along and seeing nothing but trees, rocks and an endless dusty road, I was sweaty and bored and wondering if we were wasting our time.

Then I started to notice something weird about the road. "Do you get the feeling we're riding in circles?" I asked after a long silence.

"Yeah," said Peter. "One of those long, straight circles."

"I'm serious," I said. "I don't think this road is

running straight out away from the town. I think it's curving off to the right a bit."

"So?" said Peter.

"So, I don't know yet," I murmured. "Weird though."

The conversation dropped off again for a while. A couple of times, I thought I heard the sound of other voices coming from off to our right somewhere, but I figured I was just imagining things. Then a bit further up the road, I was distracted by something glinting in the distance, breaking the monotony of the trees.

"Look." Peter pointed, noticing it too.

A big metal sign had been put up on the side of the road. We crossed over for a closer look.

"*Road work in progress*," said Peter, reading aloud. "*Authorized vehicles only. No cyclists beyond this point. For more information, call* – are they kidding? How are we going to call?"

"Can't see anything up there," said Jordan, squinting against the sun.

"Could be further up the road," Peter suggested.

"Could be nowhere at all," I said uneasily. "Could

be just a convenient way of keeping people away."

"Well, they're going to have to do better than that," said Jordan, riding on again.

We continued up the road for another hour or so, through more of the same dense bushland. My whole body ached. I was starting to think that this might not have been exactly what Dr. Montag meant by taking it easy over the weekend. Even though we were riding down a narrow road with eucalyptus trees towering on both sides, the sun still somehow managed to beat its way down to us, and we rode slower and slower as the exhaustion started to kick in.

We took a quick break for lunch, for which Jordan rationed us out one sandwich each, and then we pushed on again. I started to think I'd been right about the road work. That warning sign had turned out to be the last evidence of any human activity along the road for ages.

"It's three-thirty," said Peter after a while. "It'll take us longer to ride back than it did to get here. We should probably think about –"

"No," Jordan called back over her shoulder. "We can't go back now. We haven't found anything yet."

"We've been riding for over *three hours*," said Peter. "What if there's nothing to find? Is it really worth getting caught breaking curfew?"

"Crazy Bill wouldn't have just sent us out here for no reason," she insisted.

"Wouldn't he?" said Peter. "I mean, how do we know that? Who knows *what's* going on in that guy's head?"

"Let's give it another half an hour," I suggested. "At four o'clock, if we still haven't found anything, we can —"

"Whoa, hold on," said Jordan, suddenly skidding to a halt. She leapt from her bike and wheeled it off the road, into a little ditch at the edge of the trees.

Peter and I both froze.

"Quick!" said Jordan, frantically waving us down into the ditch with her.

We dropped our bikes and crouched low in the dirt.

Jordan stuck out a hand and pointed along the road in the direction we'd been heading. "Look," she hissed. "There's someone out there."

Chapter 22

Way off in the distance, two black-uniformed security officers were standing guard in front of a heavy boom gate that stretched out across the road. Both of them were armed. Not with the pistols that all the security guys in town kept holstered to their hips – these guys were carrying giant semi-automatic rifles.

The one closest to us was holding something up to his face.

"Binoculars," Jordan breathed. "Did they see us?"

The guard's eyes traced a wide, slow semicircle from one side of the road to the other. Then he froze, binoculars pointed almost right at us. I glanced up onto the road and a jolt of panic hit me as I realized how much dust we'd kicked up scrambling into the ditch. A big cloud of it was still hanging in the air.

The guard stared at the cloud. He straightened up and took a step towards us. I pressed my body into the dirt, silently cursing myself for not being more careful riding down the road. But a second later, the guard lowered his binoculars and slouched back down against the end of the boom gate.

"See? Nothing to worry about," said Peter, his voice a lot higher than usual. "They're just bored. I reckon the most exciting thing they've seen out here today is a kangaroo. Besides, they're just security guards. They wouldn't actually hurt us, right?"

I'm not sure who he thought he was kidding. It felt like my heart had suddenly decided to bust out of my chest and make a run for it. And, all things considered, making a run for it didn't seem like such a bad idea.

"That's weird," said Jordan, her eyes locked on the guards.

"What?"

"The security guards are only watching this end of

the road," said Jordan. "They don't seem too worried about anyone coming from the other direction."

She was right. Every now and then, one of the guards would turn and look back behind them over the boom gate, but they were clearly more interested in making sure no one got through from our side.

"They're guarding something," I whispered. I straightened up a bit higher against the wall of the ditch, trying to get a better look, but all I could see beyond the boom gate were more trees and more road. I dropped down again as one of the guards reached for something at his belt. But then he lifted his hand and I realized he was just unclipping a water bottle.

"We'll have to go around," said Jordan.

"Yeah," I said, trying to sound determined instead of terrified. "But let's leave the bikes. We'll make too much noise dragging them through the bush again."

I turned to look at Peter. His expression had suddenly shifted. Obviously his belief that the guards wouldn't hurt us was not something he wanted to test.

"You coming?" Jordan asked him.

He stared at her for a long time, then gave her a

mute little nod.

With Jordan in the lead, we left our bikes lying in the ditch and clambered up the far side. We crept about fifteen meters straight out into the bush, then veered around to the left, wanting to cut as wide a circle as possible around the security guards. But we also needed to stick close enough to the road so that we didn't lose track of how far we'd come and emerge from the trees too early. Which meant that if the guards looked hard enough, they'd probably spot us coming past.

I glanced down at my bright-red T-shirt and wished I'd been smart enough to wear clothes that would blend in with the bush. Every time my foot snapped a branch or crunched down on a leaf, I stopped dead, expecting to hear the sound of gunfire ripping through the trees.

It was a completely different kind of fear to what I'd felt at the airport with Crazy Bill. Back there, everything had happened so quickly. It was all a blur of loud noise and flashing lights with no time to absorb any of it. But here in the bush, inching our way painfully slowly between the trees, I had all the time in the world to think about how dead I would be if we were spotted.

As we passed within earshot of the guards, I caught a few snatches of their conversation.

"…not really what I had in mind when they offered me the job," one guard was saying.

"You're not wrong there," said the other. "I dragged the whole family out from Perth on the promise of a new life. And now what? I stand out here guarding an abandoned road all day."

"This is temporary though, right?" said the first guard. "I had a word with the chief, and he said in a couple of months we'll all be upgraded to more challenging work."

I glanced over at Jordan, who was biting her lip at this piece of news. I kept moving, trying not to think too hard about what this "challenging work" might involve.

Through a gap in the trees, I saw the other guard shrug. He lifted up his binoculars and started peering around into the bush again.

I crouched low behind a tree and saw Jordan and Peter do the same.

"You ever wonder what they're really doing out here?" the first guard asked. "Why they need so many of us?"

"Nope," murmured the other, his eyes sweeping across our hiding place. "Not my job to ask those sorts of questions." He dropped the binoculars again and began drumming his fingers on the butt of his rifle, staring into space.

I glanced over at Jordan and cocked my head in the direction of the guards. *Keep moving?*

She nodded and we got to our feet again.

We continued like this, parallel with the road, for another fifteen minutes or so – stopping and starting, jumping into hiding at the first sign of danger – until we were sure we'd gotten well away from the security guards.

Away from *those* security guards anyway. For all we knew, there could be a hundred more lurking around out here.

"What now?" Peter whispered. "Cut back to the road?"

"Might be safer to keep going through the bush," said Jordan. She turned to look at me. "What do you think?"

"I don't know," I said. "We'll be harder to spot in here, I guess. But so will –"

A low rumbling sound broke my train of thought.

"Do you hear that?" asked Jordan.

"Sounds like an engine," said Peter.

"Another truck?" I said, straining to hear.

"It's coming from up there," said Jordan, pointing out ahead of us.

A second later, she took off through the trees, running towards the sound.

"All right," Peter sighed. "So I guess we're giving up on the whole stealth thing."

The two of us broke into a run and started chasing after Jordan, doing our best to keep up without face-planting into a bush. In my mind, I saw security guards hiding behind every tree, waiting to jump out and start laying into us with their weapons.

Jordan leapt down into a dried-up riverbed, sprinted across it and raced up the other side. A second later, I reached the bank and found that my reflexes were not quite as quick as hers. I lost my footing and tumbled down the slope, crashing into the mess of dried leaves at the bottom. Peter hauled me to my feet and we crawled up the far bank after Jordan.

In the small corner of my brain that wasn't eaten up by fear and panic and concentrating on not stacking it again, I noticed that the rumbling seemed to be moving away to our right, like it was cutting across in front of us.

Peter and I sprinted to close up the gap between us and Jordan. She jumped a fallen log and then stopped so quickly that we almost slammed into her.

"Shh!" she hissed, as though rampaging through the bush had been our idea. She tiptoed forward and peered around a tree, into a narrow gap in the bushland.

It was another road. Not a real asphalt one like the main road out of town. This one was narrow and dusty, not much bigger than one of the bike tracks, with trees pushing in on it from both sides. Up on the left, I saw the place where it branched off the main road. The turnoff was almost completely hidden by the trees, and I doubted that we would've noticed it if we'd just been riding past.

Looking right, I saw the truck we'd heard making

its way down the road, throwing bits of gravel out behind it. The driver was taking it slow, clearly not wanting to risk slipping into a ditch or smashing his windshield against an overhanging branch.

"Where's he going?" Jordan whispered.

Peter pulled *Alice's Adventures in Wonderland* from his back pocket and opened it up. "Dunno," he said, pointing to the X that Crazy Bill had scrawled among the trees on his map. "But wherever he's headed, I reckon our mate Bill wants us to check it out."

We took a few steps back between the trees, and then started following the sound of the truck again, running alongside the road as it wound its way deeper into the bush. After all that riding, my legs felt like jelly, and pretty soon I was feeling shooting pains under my already-bruised ribs. I pressed a hand against my side and forced myself to keep moving.

After about five minutes, we heard the truck come to a stop a little way ahead of us. There were shouts, and then the sound of metal scraping against concrete – a gate opening. We crept forward, crouching down in the undergrowth, until we came to a clearing in the bush. I rubbed at the stitch in my

215

side and tried desperately to keep my breathing slow and quiet.

Stretching out across the clearing was an enormous steel-walled warehouse-type building, as big as Phoenix Mall. There were no windows as far as I could see, just a big roller-door at the front to let people in and out. The whole place was surrounded by a massive razor wire fence. I could make out four security guards patrolling outside the warehouse, all armed with the same heavy-duty weaponry as the men at the boom gate.

As we peered out through the bushes, the driver brought his truck in through a narrow pair of gates, circled around and backed up against the warehouse door. Two men climbed out of the truck, both dressed in white uniforms like the delivery men we'd seen in town the week before. The driver pulled out a blue clipboard and started talking to the nearest security guard, while the other one – a guy with a long blond ponytail – went around to open the back of the truck.

A second later, the warehouse door rolled up and the two men in white stepped inside. From our angle, it was impossible to see into the building. But the men soon reappeared, carrying a heavy wooden crate. They loaded the crate into the back of the truck, then checked their clipboard and went back into the warehouse.

"What do you think they're doing?" Peter whispered.

"Come on," said Jordan, standing up. "Let's see if we can get inside."

Chapter 23

89 DAYS

"Are you kidding?" hissed Peter. "Did you not notice the small army standing guard outside?"

"We'll go around the back," said Jordan, scrambling through the undergrowth. "See if there's another way in."

"You're insane," said Peter, but we both stood up and followed her.

I was tempted to side with Peter on this one. Surely we'd seen enough of this place without having to go *inside*. But I decided to keep my mouth shut.

We made our way along the outside of the fence, but there was no convenient back door or ventilation shaft or hole in it. Just more of the same steel walls and razor wire. Which I guess is the difference between spy movies and real life.

At least there were no security guards around this side. Not right now, anyway. Probably all distracted by the arrival of the delivery truck, but who knew how long that would last?

Jordan started pacing back and forth along the edge of the clearing, looking up into the trees. "I think maybe we could climb one of these," she said. "See how those two branches stretch right over the fence?"

Yeah, I thought. *Right into the razor wire.*

"Maybe we should head back out to the main road," I suggested. "See what the other –"

"Hold on." Jordan's eyes traced a path back down to the ground.

A big old eucalyptus tree had uprooted itself – in a storm or something, I guess – and started falling over. If it had made it all the way to the ground, it would've smashed right through the fence guarding the warehouse. But instead, it had collided with another tree and stopped mid-fall.

Jordan walked across to the half-fallen tree and

tested it with her hands. It wobbled very slightly against the other tree. I realized what she was thinking, and my heart made another escape attempt.

"Jordan!" I hissed.

"We need a diversion, don't we?" She began heaving at the side of the dead tree, slamming her full weight against the enormous trunk.

I felt the blood drain from my face. "Yeah, maybe, but –"

"Get ready to run," she warned.

"Wait!" hissed Peter urgently. "No, no, no, Jordan, stop!"

Jordan ignored him. The tree was rocking back and forth now, rolling further with each shove.

Peter took a couple of steps back into the bush. "Jordan, *please* –"

Too late.

There was a horrible, wooden creaking sound as the dead tree finally dislodged itself from the live one and continued its journey towards the ground. It crashed into the razor wire fence and kept on falling, hitting the dirt just short of the warehouse wall.

Alarms blared. Seconds later, we heard shouts and thundering footsteps from the other end of the warehouse.

"Run!" Jordan ordered.

Neither of us was about to disagree with that part of the plan. Jordan took off into the bush again, sprinting away from the fallen tree with Peter and me pounding the dirt behind her. She circled back around the warehouse, staying just far enough into the bush to avoid being seen.

A minute later, we were back at the dirt road. Jordan stopped, looked right. Then, without warning, she burst out into the clearing, running full tilt towards the open front gates.

"No," gasped Peter, sounding terrified. "We are *not —*"

But Jordan kept running. And suddenly I was running out after her. I tore straight through the gates, eyes half-closed, hands shielding my face. Any second now one of the guards would see us and I would be dead and that would be the end and then —

And then I was inside the warehouse. And I wasn't dead.

It took my panic-riddled brain a second to catch up with what had just happened. Jordan's diversion had worked. The security guards were all up at the other end of the warehouse. But they wouldn't stay there for long.

"We need to get away from the door," I said, leaning close to Jordan so she could hear me over the alarms that were still screaming out around us.

The warehouse looked even bigger from the inside. Rows of industrial shelving stretched away into the half-light, all packed full of crates and boxes. There were fluorescent tubes hanging all along the ceiling, but with no windows anywhere they made the floor below look even more dim and shadowy.

We moved clear of the doorway and turned down one of the long aisles between two lines of shelves. A metal sign hung in the air at the top of the aisle, stamped with a big number three and the words, *MALL SUPPLY – GENERAL*.

The shelves towered over us, pressing in from both sides, making the whole place feel somehow huge and claustrophobic at the same time.

I kept glancing back over my shoulder, positive

that we were digging our own graves deeper with every step. The guards would be back any minute now, and then we'd be trapped in here. And with the alarms still going off all over the place, we wouldn't even hear them coming.

Up ahead, a cardboard box had fallen from a shelf and was lying open on its side, spilling a pile of clothes onto the floor. As we got closer I saw that they were red skirts, all identical.

"School uniforms," said Jordan, picking one of them up. She turned it over in her hands, like she was checking it was the real deal, then dropped it back on top of the pile.

Peter was scanning the shelves behind her. He whispered something in her ear and pointed at the shelf that the box of skirts had fallen from. There were hundreds of other boxes up there, all neatly labeled.

P.H.S. Collared Shirts – LS (M)

P.H.S. Collared Shirts – LS (F)

P.H.S. Trousers

P.H.S. Polyester Ties (Red)

Enough to keep the whole school stocked up for about a million years.

But it wasn't just school stuff. Crammed along the shelves below were boxes stuffed with everything from jeans to tuxedos – supplies of what looked like every piece of clothing sold at Phoenix Mall.

We kept moving and a few seconds later we realized that clothes were only the beginning. Further down the aisle were shelves piled up with toys and board games and sports equipment. Then there were boxes of paper cups and plastic spoons and sugar packets and napkins and cans of drinking chocolate and giant bags of coffee beans. And more and more stuff after that, and this was just the first aisle we'd looked down.

I stopped walking. The alarms were still blaring, but I barely even noticed them anymore. "This is … *everything*, isn't it?" I said. "All of our stuff. Everything that's getting brought into town by those delivery trucks. It's all coming from –" I gestured weakly at the piles of stuff all around us. "None of it's coming from outside, is it? It's all from … from here."

"No," said Peter. He was trying to sound determined, but his voice was even shakier than mine. "No, come on, it's not – it's some kind of temporary storage facility, right? For, like, overflow from the mall. They bring the supplies in from the outside and then store them here until we need them in town." He shook his head. "This is just – this is normal."

"Guarding coffee cups with semi-automatic weapons?" I snapped. "You think that's normal?"

It seemed like the more scared I got, the less patience I had for Peter's obsessive attempts to deny what was right in front of him.

"Look at this," Jordan whispered, stopping Peter before he could answer. She reached down and picked something up from one of the shelves.

It was a copy of *Time* magazine. The man on the cover had graying hair, a warm smile, and skin that looked like it had been stretched a bit too tightly across his face. Underneath was a heading that read, *Noah Shackleton: Building a Better Tomorrow.*

"Mr. Shackleton," said Peter. "So what?"

"Look at the date," she said, stabbing a finger down at the corner of the page.

July 20.

We were only halfway through May.

"There are others, too." Jordan stuck the

magazine in her bag and started pacing along the shelf. *"Reader's Digest, Money, Cosmo, New Scientist…* There are copies here right up to the middle of August."

A fresh wave of panic hit me as I put two and two together. "Right up until Tabitha," I said.

I picked up one of the magazines and flipped through it, fighting to keep my hands steady. Everything inside looked completely legit. But it was all fake. All of this. The supply trucks and the delivery people and this warehouse and these magazines and all of this stuff…

"We're completely cut off, aren't we?" I said, turning to look at Jordan. "There's nothing –"

My words were suddenly ten times louder in my ears. I slammed my mouth shut. The alarms had just cut out across the warehouse.

A second later, a muffled voice echoed down our aisle from the other end of the building.

Peter swore under his breath.

The security guys were back inside. And they were coming this way.

Chapter 24

"How exactly were you planning on getting us *out* of here when the guys with guns came back?" Peter muttered to Jordan as we ran the rest of the way down the aisle and slipped around the corner to hide.

"We'll figure something out," said Jordan, which wasn't exactly an answer.

"Right," said Peter through gritted teeth. "Fantastic."

Peering through the gap between a couple of crates, I saw two men appear at the other end of the aisle we'd just left. The delivery guy with the clipboard and one of the security guards.

"No worries," Clipboard Guy was saying, "we'll notify maintenance when we get back – get Ketterley to send a couple of guys over."

"You two want a hand loading the truck?"

"Nah, we'll be all right. Not much on the list today."

"Ah well … might as well grab a drink while I'm in here."

"Hey, you know you're not meant to take any of this without –"

"Yeah, yeah," said the security guy dismissively. "Come on, who's gonna know?"

Clipboard Guy took another look down at his clipboard and the two of them started moving up the aisle, obviously searching the shelves for something on their list. They hadn't seen us, but for a minute I just stood there, glued to the spot, watching them come closer.

"C'mon," Peter whispered, yanking at my arm.

Jordan had just checked down the next aisle to make sure the coast was clear and was creeping out along the back wall of the warehouse. We followed her, trying to stay in the shadows.

It was stop-start all the way. Pause at the top of each aisle. Check for guards. Race across to the cover of the next row of shelves. Which, I reminded myself, would be no cover at all if any of the guards made it up to our end of the warehouse.

About halfway along, we came to an aisle with a clear line of sight all the way through to the front entrance. Sure enough, the guards were back on patrol, blocking our way out of here. It seemed like our only option would be to find somewhere to hide until… Until what? They had to be guarding this place twenty-four seven.

We bolted across the gap and stopped dead. In the next aisle, the guy with the ponytail was struggling to bring an enormous box down from a shelf above his head.

"Mitch?" he said as we dashed past behind him. Risking a look back through a gap in the shelves, I saw him stare up at our end of the aisle, a suspicious look on his face. But his box was already halfway off the shelf, tipping down towards him. "Hey, Mitch, give me a hand with the toilet paper, will you?"

"He really should be able to take care of that

himself by now," Peter muttered nervously as we moved on again.

A few seconds later, there was a loud crash behind us. I heard Ponytail shout.

"You all right, mate?" called Clipboard Guy from across the warehouse, and suddenly there were footsteps thundering towards us.

Time to run.

We raced to the end of the warehouse and dashed into the last aisle, just in time to avoid being spotted by the two men as they rounded the corner behind us. This aisle was almost empty, except for a few bikes standing at the end of a long metal rack on the bottom shelf. And one security guard.

I staggered, only just managing to keep myself from shouting out. We were twenty meters apart, if that. It was a miracle he hadn't heard us coming. But the guard was facing the other direction, walking away from us.

We dived down behind the bikes and waited for him to leave. I could feel the blood pounding in my ears and I grabbed onto the bike tire in front of me for support, struggling to hold still. But I couldn't move either, couldn't even breathe, because if he turned around…

From a few aisles down, I heard Clipboard Guy's voice and the sound of boxes being shifted. The guard in front of us started walking more quickly.

Yes, I thought. *Go. Keep moving. Go help them.*

After one excruciating minute, he reached the end of the aisle and disappeared. I heaved a sigh and felt my muscles relax very slightly.

"Hey, look!" hissed Jordan, getting to her feet again. She started backtracking along the row of shelves towards a shadowy corner at the back of the warehouse, where a concrete staircase led down into the ground, disappearing into the darkness.

Checking for guards one last time, Jordan darted out and made a break for the stairs. Peter looked like he wanted to argue with her, but he just rolled his eyes and followed her down.

It was almost pitch black at the bottom of the stairs. I took one step too many and nearly rolled my ankle on the dusty floor. Up ahead, there was a narrow strip of light shining out from under a door. Jordan fumbled for the handle and pulled it open.

Bright light burned my eyes. I ducked down,

blinded, waiting for the shout of a guard or the ringing of an alarm. But the only sound I heard was Peter pulling the door shut behind us. It seemed like we were alone down here.

I knew that we needed to keep moving, but for a minute all I could do was stand there, squinting stupidly, waiting for my vision to return. At first I couldn't see anything but white light and a sea of green.

Then the room slowly came into focus and I realized that the green things were plants. Vegetables. Thousands of them.

The room we'd stumbled into was just as big as the warehouse above it. The whole place was packed with row after row of waist-high tables covered in leafy green plants. Instead of soil, the plants were suspended across clear plastic trays, roots dangling down into a cloudy white liquid like flour in water. Black hoses snaked all over the place, pumping the liquid around, and light beamed down on the plants from low-hanging lamps.

"Whoa," said Peter. "It's a hydroponics bay."

"A what?" I said, glancing at him.

"For growing plants without any soil or sunlight,"

said Peter. "You know, like in *Star Trek*."

"Also like in *real life*," said Jordan, raising an eyebrow at him. "I guess this is where all our fresh food is coming from."

We started making our way between the rows of vegetables. Not that we really had any idea where we were going, but it seemed like a good idea to keep moving. Looking around, I saw fruit trees growing along the walls using an upsized version of the same technology.

"I don't get it," I said, staring around at the endless green. "Why do we need all of this?"

Jordan shrugged. "People need to eat."

"Yeah, but they've got everything else stored in that warehouse – surely they could get veggies in from outside?"

"Maybe it's not just for now," Jordan said quietly. "Maybe they need something more long-lasting for, you know, *after*."

In the far corner of the hydroponics bay was a little glass-walled room filled with computers – some kind of control station, maybe – and racks and tables piled up with gardening equipment.

Empty crates and boxes were stacked all along the back wall, waiting to be packed full of vegetables and sent upstairs. But there was no way a crate that big was fitting up the staircase we'd come down on. Which meant that there had to be another way out of here.

"There's an elevator," said Jordan, noticing it a split second before I did. She walked over and pushed the button on the wall. The doors opened instantly, and she and I stepped inside.

"Hang on a minute," said Peter, holding the elevator door. "You sure you want to go bursting out there?"

"What, you want to stay down here forever?" Jordan asked him.

"No. But I don't want to get *shot* either."

"You have another suggestion?" she asked.

Peter looked like he definitely had another suggestion for where Jordan could stick her idea, but I guess he figured she wouldn't go for it. Without saying anything, he stepped into the elevator with Jordan and me and pushed the ground floor button.

The elevator clattered to life – way too noisily –

and started rolling its way up to the warehouse level. I shrank back from the doors as we rose, half-expecting to find a bunch of rifles trained on us as soon as the doors opened again. We came to a stop and I spun around as a second set of doors clanked apart behind me.

A wire fence and a sea of trees. We were back outside.

I struggled to get my bearings. For a second, I wondered why we hadn't noticed the elevator doors when we'd first arrived, but then I figured that we were around the opposite side of the warehouse from the one we'd come in on. There were no security guards in sight, although that could change any second.

"Which way?" I asked.

"Around the back," Jordan whispered, after thinking about it for a minute. "Out through the hole in the fence."

Peter and I both nodded. It was either that or the front gate, and we *knew* we weren't getting out of that one alive. We crept away from the elevator and raced towards the back end of the warehouse.

The sun was just starting to set, but not nearly

enough for the darkness to give us any protection. As we reached the end of the building, Jordan raised a hand into the air to signal us to stop. She peered around the corner, then snapped her head back again and said, "We're clear."

"Roger that, commander," Peter smirked.

I followed them across to the fallen tree and realized right away that escaping through the fence wasn't going to be as simple as I'd imagined.

When the tree fell, it hadn't knocked the fence all the way down, but it hadn't torn a neat hole either. The fence had buckled around the trunk, bending forward so that the razor wire on top was jutting out towards us.

To get out, we'd have to climb onto the fallen tree, crawl across the narrow gap it had plowed through the razor wire – without slipping off and getting ripped to shreds – and then jump down into the bush.

All without getting captured or shot.

Now that we were right up against the tree, its branches and leaves were providing us with at least a bit of cover. But I doubted that it would make a difference if one of the guards came strolling around the corner.

"Who's going first?" I asked.

Peter glanced back and forth between me and the fence, clearly wanting to get out of here as fast as possible, but not game to be the first one to test the strength of the tree.

"I'll go," said Jordan, unsurprisingly.

She pulled herself up on top of the fallen tree, straddling the trunk, and started shuffling her way across to the other side. From the other end of the compound, I heard the delivery truck rev into life. Any second now, it would be out of here and we'd lose any advantage that distraction might be giving us.

I jogged back over to the corner of the warehouse to make sure there was still no one coming. All clear so far.

Jordan was making quick progress on the tree, and it seemed like it was stable enough, so Peter clambered on behind her. But Peter was heavier than Jordan and not as nimble, and the leaves around him shook noisily each time he moved.

I shot him a look, urging him to be more quiet, but he shrugged his shoulders, like, *What do you want me to do about it?*

I stuck my head back around the corner, then jerked it back again so quickly I almost fell over. Two of the guards were headed this way. So far they were just patrolling, wandering along, but any minute now they'd get close enough to hear all the noise we were making.

"Someone's coming!" I hissed, racing back towards the fallen tree. Peter gave up any attempt at going slow and steady, and started clawing desperately at the branches up ahead of him. As soon as there was room behind Peter, I climbed up and started crawling across.

The sound of the truck's engine faded away behind us and I heard the distant scraping of the gate being dragged shut. Jordan was almost over the fence by now. She'd cleared the razor wire and was twisting her way between two giant branches that stuck out in front of her. Peter wasn't far behind. His shoulder jolted back suddenly and he grunted in pain as a stray bit of razor wire caught on his arm. I tried to go faster, to close the gap between me and Peter. Leaves and twigs jutted out all around me, poking at the bruises on my face.

With a muffled thud, Jordan dropped to her feet

on the far side of the fence. She stretched out a hand, ready to help Peter across. He glanced back at me and I would've laughed at the look on his face if I wasn't so busy *not* getting killed. I reached the edge of the razor wire and pressed down on a sturdy-looking branch for support.

CRACK!

The branch turned out to be not so sturdy. As soon as I put my weight on top of it, it dropped and went tumbling down to the ground, landing with a crash of leaves. I staggered forward, caught myself against the trunk, and narrowly avoided plunging into the razor wire.

But the damage was done. I heard a distant shout followed closely by footsteps that definitely wouldn't be distant for long. Up ahead, I saw Jordan hauling Peter down to the ground. He landed on all fours and sprang to his feet.

I glanced back over my shoulder and then dived the rest of the way through the razor wire, making a desperate grab at one of the big branches I'd seen Jordan weaving through before. My fingers brushed against the branch, but then my jeans snagged on the wire and I crashed down hard against the tree, my already-bruised face hitting the trunk. I closed my eyes, head spinning.

"Come on!" Peter hissed, his eyes flashing back to the warehouse.

The guards had to be right behind me now. I dragged myself up again, fighting to get my breath back. Finally, my leg came free and I tumbled to the ground in a heap. I heard a shout from above me – Peter or one of the guards, I couldn't tell which – then two hands grabbed hold of me and dragged me to my feet. Jordan.

I stumbled, vision still hazy. She grabbed my hand, pulling me forward, and the three of us dashed away into the bush.

Chapter 25

"Never again," Peter panted. "Never. Not ever."

He sounded half-delirious. Not that I could blame him.

"Did they see us?" I gasped, as we stumbled through the bush, putting some distance between us and the warehouse. I was walking in a straight line again, but the last five minutes were still a total blur.

"I don't know," said Jordan, looking back. "No. I don't think so."

I realized I was still holding on to her hand and quickly dropped it.

"No guns," said Peter vaguely.

"Huh?"

"They didn't shoot us," he said. "And they didn't seem like the kind of guys who'd hold back if they saw a trespasser."

"Yeah, right," I nodded wearily. The guards had definitely heard something, but it looked like we'd gotten away. I came to a stop and grabbed onto a tree for support. "So, now what?"

"It's five o'clock," said Peter, staring up at the sky. "We need to get back to our bikes if we want a hope of getting home before curfew."

"Not yet we don't," said Jordan. "We're only half-finished."

"Are you kidding?" said Peter. "No. No way. We are *all* finished."

"What about the other place on Crazy Bill's map?"

"You know what?" Peter snapped. "I reckon I've had about enough of Crazy Bill's surprises for one day."

"But –"

"Look," he said, stabbing a finger at her. "You want to spend the night out here? You want to go find more opportunities to get shot at? Be my guest. But you can count me out of it."

It was surprising to hear Peter speak to Jordan like that, and he looked like maybe he regretted saying it. But he was at least as scared as I was, and I guess that fear was finally starting to outweigh his desire to stay on Jordan's good side.

"Fine," said Jordan, turning to look at me. "You coming, Luke?"

I didn't answer right away.

"Mate, come on," said Peter, obviously not liking the thought of making the journey home by himself. "Haven't we been through enough for one day? If we decide we want to come back some other time –"

Jordan muttered something under her breath.

"Sorry, *what?*" said Peter, stepping up until they were nose to nose.

"I said, as if you'd ever come back again!"

"What's that supposed to mean?"

"It means if you don't even have the guts to come

with us now, then as if we'll ever convince you to –"

"Oh, right," said Peter, rolling his eyes, "so just because I don't want to give you another chance to get us all killed, that makes me a coward, does it?"

Jordan stared coldly at him, letting the question hang in the air for a minute. "No," she said, "deliberately blocking your ears to the truth is what makes you a coward."

Peter glared at her. "That is *not* fair. If either of you can show me one piece of *concrete* evidence –"

"Don't give me that," spat Jordan. "This has nothing to do with evidence and you know it! You just don't *want* any of it to be true, because then you might actually have to step up and do something about it!"

Peter said nothing. He just stood there, shaking his head, too furious to even speak. I tried to step in, but Jordan wouldn't let me get a word in edgewise.

"And that scares you doesn't it, Weir?" she plowed on. "So instead of facing facts, you just invent your own little fantasy world where this is a joke and you can keep living your pathetic little –"

"Jordan…" I said.

"Sure, seven billion people might be about to get murdered, but what does that matter so long as Peter Weir can keep on deluding himself that everything's –"

"Jordan," I repeated. "*Stop.*"

She stopped.

I closed my eyes. The painkillers had well and truly worn off by now. As if I didn't have enough to worry about without trying to stop these two from ripping each other to pieces. Not that there wasn't a bit of truth in what Jordan had said, but now was clearly not the time to be having that discussion.

Both of them were staring at me when I opened my eyes again.

"I want to go home," I said.

"Luke," Jordan began.

"I want to go home right now and crawl into my bed and forget that this ever happened. But then what?"

Peter shot me a look like he was trying to figure out whose side I was on.

"Jordan's right," I continued. "If we go home now, we're not coming back. No way am I going through all this again. So we need to decide whether we're going to do this or not. And we need to do it without screaming so loud that everyone within a million kilometers can hear where we are."

"I don't care what you do," said Jordan, pulling her backpack up over her shoulder and turning to walk away. "I'm going."

"No, Jordan," I said firmly.

Jordan stopped in her tracks, but didn't turn around.

"Either we all agree to this, or we turn back and go home," I said, with no idea how I would enforce that if either of them wanted to challenge me. "I'm not letting you go running off by yourself over some stupid argument."

"You're *not letting* me?"

Suddenly, she was back in my face again. I braced myself for whatever onslaught was coming next. But then she looked me right in the eye and her expression shifted.

I don't know whether it was because she'd used up all her energy on Peter, or if she caught sight of the damage Crazy Bill had already done to me and decided

I'd suffered enough. But *something* happened, because the anger suddenly evaporated from her face and when she spoke again, her voice was much calmer.

"Okay," she breathed. "What do you want to do?"

"I don't know," I admitted. "I'm scared and I'm tired and I don't even want to think about what else might be out here. But if we decide to keep going, I'll keep going."

Jordan smiled.

"All right, let's get moving then," said Peter, stepping between us.

Jordan stared at him like he was up to something. "You're the one who –"

He sighed heavily. "We're screwed either way, aren't we? Even if we make it home without running into any more security, we're still gonna get busted for breaking curfew. If I'm gonna die, I might as well do it making you happy."

We cut back across through the trees and eventually found our way to the main road again. We walked along by the side of the road, ready to duck for cover at the first sign of trouble, but I had a feeling there was less chance of anyone coming past now that we were away from the warehouse.

The sky was changing color and our shadows were getting longer, but there was still plenty of light. None of us talked very much for a while. I guess we were all still calming down after our little blowup back in the bush. Jordan passed around the rest of the sandwiches from her bag as we walked, and I suddenly realized I was starving.

It was much slower going without our bikes and, as the sun continued to drift downward, I was reminded of all the movies I'd seen where wandering backpackers got dragged off deserted roads by bloodthirsty psychopaths. I tried to tell myself that the only bloodthirsty psychopath I knew was locked up in town, but somehow that didn't make me feel any better.

A bit further down the road, we saw a set of tire tracks veering off through the dirt to our right and disappearing into the bush – too small to have been made by one of the delivery trucks, but probably too big for a car. They looked recent, but in the end we decided not to check them out – they'd be impossible to follow through the bush and Crazy Bill's map seemed pretty clear that whatever we were looking for was *on* the road. Or so we thought.

"Look up there," I said after about half an hour of walking. "Trees."

"Yep," said Peter. "They're a prominent feature out here."

"No, I mean up there in front of us." I jogged ahead of the others to see where the road was taking us next. "It must veer off in another direction."

But a minute later I got close enough to realize that this road wasn't veering anywhere. "Uh, guys?" I called, looking back.

"What is it?" said Jordan, coming up behind me. "Did you find –"

She and Peter reached the place where I was standing and stopped in their tracks.

"Oh."

"Yeah," said Peter. "This is probably not a good sign."

Chapter 26

About ten meters up ahead, the road came to an end.

Not like a real dead end, with a warning sign and a place to do a U-turn or whatever. It just faded away into the grass, like whoever was building it had suddenly gone, "Forget this!" and walked off the job.

For a few minutes we just stood there, gazing at the ground. The words *dead end* rattled around in my brain. Because this was it. The end. This was where they gave up pretending. This was the place where the carefully constructed lie that Phoenix was just an ordinary town stopped getting told. No one was supposed to make it this far.

Eventually Peter blew out a lungful of air and said, "What now?"

"I dunno," I said, scanning the bush around us for some sign of … anything. "I guess this is it, right? This is what Crazy Bill wanted us to see."

Jordan reached over and pulled *Alice's Adventures in Wonderland* out of Peter's pocket.

"Maybe not," she said, flipping to the map and pointing. "That's the place we're heading for, right? We were assuming it was on the road, but look – there's a gap between the end of that line and the X. What if the thing we're meant to see is still out there somewhere?"

"I think maybe you're reading too much into it," said Peter. "I don't reckon Crazy Bill was paying a whole lot of attention to detail when he drew this."

"Might as well keep going though, now that we're here," I said, seeing Jordan's nostrils flare and wanting to avoid another argument. "No point leaving without making sure."

But I was pretty sure Peter was right. As much as I wanted to think there could be something else out here, I couldn't see what Jordan was hoping to find.

Peter sighed and led the way past the end of the road. Jordan shoved the book into her bag and the two of us followed him into the bush.

It was suddenly darker now that we were back under the cover of the trees, and I found myself stumbling in the undergrowth a lot more than before, struggling to figure out what was real and what was shadow before I stepped on it and it was too late.

After twenty minutes, I was just about ready to start heading back. We'd already lost all hope of beating curfew, and I wanted at least to be back on the road again before darkness surrounded us completely.

Peter was looking fed up too, but he didn't say anything. His eyes kept darting over to Jordan every few seconds, but he'd given up on his angry glares and was back to his usual habit of just looking at her for the sake of looking at her. I wondered whether some of what she'd said to him before had made an impact.

I gave it another five minutes, just to satisfy Jordan that there was nothing else out here, and then reached out and put a hand on her shoulder.

"What is it?" she said, turning around. "Did you find something?"

I shook my head. "Jordan, listen. I think maybe we've already found everything there is to find."

"No," Jordan insisted. "This can't be all. We didn't come all the way out here just to –"

"Hey, what's that?" said Peter, stopping up ahead of us. He'd just sidestepped between two giant gum trees, and I had to follow him through before I could see what he was looking at.

Up ahead, maybe fifty meters away, something huge and gray stretched out in front of us. It rose up as far as I could see through the trees and seemed to spread out to the left and right.

Jordan put a finger to her lips, crouched low and began creeping forward. Peter and I followed along behind. My eyes darted through the shadows, scanning for any sign of movement.

A little bush rat bounced across our path and I almost had a heart attack. But if security were out here, they were keeping quiet.

We reached the expanse of gray and I pressed a hand against its surface. It was a wall. Solid concrete, towering up almost as high as the trees around it. Jordan flicked on the flashlight from her bag and started shining it around the wall, trying to figure out how big it was.

"It's another building, right?" Peter frowned, staring up at it. "Another storage facility."

"Yeah, maybe." I stood back a bit to see if I could spot a way inside. But there was nothing.

"Maybe it's a hangar," said Peter. "What if this is where they're storing all the helicopters and stuff that they moved away from the airport?"

There was a rustling behind me and I spun around. "Where's Jordan?"

Peter glanced away from the wall and pointed off to his side. "She's just –"

But he was pointing into empty space.

I stared around at the trees, shifting my weight from foot to foot, wanting to go looking for her, but having no idea which direction to run in.

"Jordan!" Peter called, stumbling through the bush. "Jor– !"

"Peter, stop!" I hissed. "What if –"

I heard the sound of footsteps approaching, crunching through the dead leaves. Seconds later, light flickered through the bushes and Jordan came bursting back out towards us. She raised an eyebrow at our panicked expressions.

"What's wrong?" she panted.

Peter shot her an exasperated look. "Jordan – don't *do* that!"

"Do what?"

"Don't go running off into the bush without us!" he said. "You could have been –"

"I'm fine," she said dismissively. "Just having a look further down."

"And?" I said.

"I can't see any way in," she said with a shrug. "And I can't find the end either. Whatever this thing is, it's big." She leaned back against the wall and stared up into the trees.

"So is that it?" said Peter hopefully. "Are we done here? I mean, if we can't find a way around this thing…"

"Yeah," said Jordan, "I guess we'll have to go over it."

"See anything yet?" I called.

"Not yet," said Jordan. "Nearly there, though."

It had taken her about fifteen minutes to find a tree she was happy with, but now Jordan had almost climbed up high enough to look over the top of the wall. Slung over her shoulder was the big coil of rope that had been taking up half the space in her backpack all afternoon. She'd been smart to bring that stuff with her after all.

I stood at the bottom of the tree, holding Jordan's bag and shining the flashlight up at her so she could see where she was going.

"Are you okay?" I asked. "Can you see?"

"Yeah, fine." She squinted as the beam flashed across her face.

"We don't *all* have to climb up there, right?" I said to Peter as I flicked off the flashlight.

"After everything that's happened today, you're worried about climbing a tree?"

"No," I said. "I'm worried about *falling* from a tree."

I peered up. Jordan crouched on a branch that was level with the top of the wall, and found the end of her rope. Leaning against the tree like she was giving it a hug, she passed the rope around between her hands and tied it off in a big loop around the trunk. She pulled at the rope, testing that it was secure, and then stood up again.

Just watching her up that high was enough to turn my stomach.

The branch Jordan was standing on ran all the way to the wall, its leaves splaying out across the concrete. She began slowly edging away from the trunk, eyes fixed on her feet. She held the rope with both hands, releasing it a bit at a time as she went along.

As she stepped out further from the trunk, I noticed the branch beginning to wobble slightly under her feet.

"Careful," I called up.

"Yeah, good," muttered Peter. "Bet she hadn't thought of that."

Jordan continued along the branch until she was right up against the concrete. She slung the rest of the rope back over her shoulder and reached one hand at a time up to the top of the wall. With a grunt, she hoisted herself over the edge and out of sight.

I stood back, staring up into the air. "Jordan?"

There was a long silence. Then Jordan's head

appeared over the top of the wall.

"What do you see?" Peter asked.

"This thing is like two meters thick!" she called. "There's no way anything is –"

She broke off, gazing out between the treetops. When she spoke again, her voice was hollow. "Guys, get up here."

I craned my neck, staring up through the mess of branches. "I don't know if I can –"

"No. Seriously. Get up here."

I looked at Peter.

"C'mon," he grunted, pulling himself up onto one of the lower branches.

I pulled Jordan's backpack up over my shoulders. "All right," I sighed. "But if I break my legs, you're carrying me home."

I navigated my way up the tree much more slowly than Jordan had done. My mind kept flashing back to the snapping branch back at the warehouse that had almost killed us all, and I tested each foothold three times before I put my full weight on it.

Peter started out pretty confidently, scrambling up ahead of me like we were having a race. He peered down at me through the branches, grinning smugly, and I got the feeling he was trying to make up for all the arguing before by impressing Jordan with his tree-climbing ability.

He slowed down as he hit the narrower branches though, and got to the top only a little way ahead of me. Grabbing hold of the rope, he started shuffling towards Jordan. I pulled myself up onto the branch just as Peter climbed off the other end.

"No," he whispered, standing up. "How can that – there's no way…" His voice was low and shaky.

I turned around to see what he was looking at, but I still wasn't up high enough. "What is it?" I called to him.

No answer.

Gritting my teeth, I clutched the rope and stepped out from the tree. There were no other strong branches within reach, nothing to hold on to for support except the rope. I edged my way along, much more slowly than the others. Something was shaking. I couldn't tell if it was me or the branch. Balance has never been my strong point and by the time I got up on the top, my body was so flooded with adrenaline that I had to grab Jordan's arm for support.

What I saw next didn't help.

It was dark by now, but not dark enough to disguise what this wall was or just how far it stretched out on either side of us.

The wall was big. Impossibly big. And it wasn't the side of a building. It was a barrier. A blockade. It stretched around the bushland in a giant ring, kilometers across. There were no gaps, no breaks, no doors.

Just one massive, unbroken circle of three-story-tall, two-meter-thick concrete.

And Phoenix was right in the middle.

Chapter 27

"This is … not possible," Peter muttered, sitting down on top of the wall.

"Yeah," I said shakily. "Except we're looking at it."

I peered over the far edge of the wall, hoping desperately for some sign of life – a road or a town or even a beaten-down old farmhouse. But there was nothing out there. Nothing but barren, rocky wasteland as far as I could see. Even the trees seemed to fade away on this side of the barrier.

I felt sick.

We'd known from the beginning that Phoenix was isolated. And getting in touch with the outside world had never seemed like an easy prospect.

But this was different. We weren't just isolated. We were trapped.

Even if we got down there – even if we packed food and supplies and somehow got our bikes over the wall – chances were we'd starve to death before we hit civilization. And there'd still be the small matter of the end of the world to deal with.

I watched Jordan, standing with her hands on her hips, looking out at the sunset. She had a defeated expression on her face that I'd never seen before, and I suddenly realized how much my own confidence had been depending on hers.

"What do you want to do now?" I asked her.

For a long time, she didn't answer. She just stared out into the wasteland.

"Jordan?"

She balled up her fists and made a noise like an angry lion. "What was the point of sending us out here?" she shouted. "I thought we came out here to find *answers* to all of this!"

"We got 'em," Peter murmured from his perch on the wall. "They just weren't the answers we wanted."

He was staring down at the town, but his face was blank, like he didn't have enough energy left to even focus his eyes.

He'd finally cracked. He'd finally found something that was just too big for his denial. The truth that Jordan and I had been trying to get our heads around bit by bit for the last week and a half was all crashing down on him at once.

The wind was starting to pick up. I sat down too, afraid of being blown off balance, and gazed back over Phoenix. I could see a glow coming up from among the trees in the middle of the circle, but only the Shackleton Building reached above the tree line.

I'd been right about the road, I realized. Not that I could see much of it from here, but Phoenix was far too close for us to have been riding out from it in a straight line all this time. They must have built the road in a spiral out from the town, deliberately making it as long as they could to keep people from coming out this far.

"It's not just Calvin, is it?" I said. "It's not just a few people who are planning all this. This wall – I mean, Calvin didn't just build it all while the rest of the town wasn't looking. This Tabitha thing goes all the way to the top."

Peter nodded, his face white.

I guess I'd halfway figured that out already. But it was one thing to suspect it, and another thing altogether to have the truth sledgehammered into my face like this. My mind raced in circles, trying to come to grips with everything that had happened today. But it was all just a blur. Just noise. Too much to process.

I closed my eyes, trying to block it all out. But unfortunately, *there's no place like home* doesn't work in real life.

"What do you reckon this is?" said Peter hoarsely, bringing me back to reality.

He was running his hand across the concrete in front of him. A metal groove, maybe ten centimeters wide, ran along the length of the wall, dividing it down the middle. As far as I could tell, it went all the way around the circle.

"Some kind of reinforcement, maybe?" I suggested. Not that there was anything in Phoenix that two meters of solid concrete needed reinforcing against.

"Yeah," said Peter, unconvinced, but not really seeming to care that much. "Maybe."

"We should go," said Jordan, finally turning to face us. "Get back down, try to get to our bikes. Should be easier to get past the guards now that it's dark. We'll still have the security in town to deal with, but –"

"Jordan, look!" Peter had suddenly jumped to his feet. He grabbed Jordan's arm and pointed down into the wasteland beyond the outside of the wall.

Two bright spots, moving side by side.

Headlights. There was someone out there.

"They're coming closer," said Jordan, and I could hear the life rushing back into her voice. "We've got to get down there!"

She bent down and started pulling off her shoes. "Get your socks," she said frantically.

I stared blankly at her.

"For the friction." She pulled off her socks and started putting her shoes back on over her bare feet. "Your hands'll get ripped to pieces otherwise."

Not the most helpful explanation.

"Why would I –?"

"Just hurry up and do it!"

She laced up her shoes in about two seconds, and started pulling her socks on over her hands. Then she picked up the coil of rope, threw it down over the far side of the wall, and I finally figured out what she was doing.

"No, Jordan, we can't," I said weakly, but I was ripping off my shoes at the same time.

Jordan grabbed the rope with both hands, pulling it tight, and leaned out away from the tree, feet perched on the far edge of the wall. I looked out past her feet, but it was too dark to see the ground. The wall below her faded away into black.

"Are you sure that rope is strong enough?" I asked, my eyes darting back to the tree.

"Should be," she said, giving it another tug. "We'll find out in a minute though, huh?"

Grinning a bit at the look on my face, she glanced into the darkness below her, crouched low, and stepped down over the edge.

I heard a series of grunts and shuffling noises as Jordan slid down the rope, then a dull thud and a loud, "Wh –? *Oomph!*"

Then nothing.

Peter grabbed the flashlight – which I'd completely forgotten was shoved into the side pocket of my jeans – and shone it down over Jordan.

"You okay?" he called down.

"Yeah," said Jordan, getting to her feet and squinting back at us. "Rough landing, though. Rope's not quite long enough. Here, throw that and my bag down to me, will you?"

She held out her hands to catch the flashlight, flipped it round, and shone it up into our faces.

"Come on – quick!" she said, throwing a glance out behind her. The headlights were still there, still coming closer. But there was nothing to stop them veering away again at any moment.

Wrapping my socks around my hands, I grabbed onto the rope and sat down on the edge of the wall. Another gust of wind blasted past, almost knocking me off. I steadied myself with the rope, my heart hammering in my ears.

"Just slide down," said Jordan, halfway between encouraging and impatient. "You'll be fine as long as you don't let go of the rope."

"Uh-huh," I murmured, wondering whether passing out might not be such a bad idea after all, because at least then I'd be unconscious when I hit the ground.

I closed my eyes and slipped down over the edge with my back against the wall.

It was all over in seconds. I gripped the rope as hard as I could, but still couldn't keep it from running away through my hands. I slid down towards the ground, bumping into the wall as I went, concrete pulling up my shirt and scraping against my back. And then suddenly I was at the end of the rope. I fell through the air for half a second, crashed down hard into a scraggly bush, then rolled away and staggered to my feet just in time to keep Peter from landing on top of me.

"Next time, we bring a ladder," he muttered, standing up and examining the scratches on his arms.

"Where are they?" I said.

Jordan spun me around and I saw the headlights moving along to our left. They were close now, maybe a hundred meters away, but it was still hard to tell whether they were purposely headed for Phoenix or not. The vehicle moved slowly, twisting and turning as it navigated its way across the rough terrain.

We took off at a run, chasing after it, Jordan out in front with the flashlight. There was no time to think, no time to do anything but keep running after those two beams of light – the closest thing to a sign of hope that we'd seen since we set out.

The landscape was completely different out here – harsh and dry and spotted with wiry half-dead grass. Either the bushland around Phoenix had all been planted, or else someone had razed all the ground out here.

"Hey!" yelled Jordan as we sprinted forward. "Hey, over here!"

We cut across to intercept the vehicle, closing in just as it reached the wall.

Peter and I joined in the shouting. "Hey, you! Wait! Stop!"

The headlights slowed. I thought I could make out the shape of a big four-wheel-drive behind them, but we were still too far away to tell. The driver wheeled around until the lights were shining right into our faces, and then cut the engine.

The door opened and a man jumped out, silhouetted against the headlights. He strode towards us, reaching for something at his hip. A chill shot through me as the man's face came into view.

It was Officer Reeve.

Chapter 28

"Stay right where you are," Officer Reeve ordered, training his gun on us. He was holding it in one hand, the other one still bound up in a sling. "Keep your hands – oh." He realized who we were and lowered the weapon.

I was shaking. "Officer Reeve –"

"How did you three get out here?" he demanded, cutting me short. His expression was suddenly very cold.

"Us?" said Peter. "How did you get out here with a *car?"*

Officer Reeve didn't answer. He holstered his

weapon and rubbed a hand down over his face.

"No one is supposed to…" he stopped and shook his head, then unclipped a set of keys from his belt. "Follow me."

He led us around behind his vehicle, which turned out to be some kind of armored van. It was all black, with a Shackleton crest on the side.

"What are you doing out here?" Peter asked.

Again, Officer Reeve ignored him. He pulled out a key and opened up the back of the van. "Get in," he said.

"But –"

"If you want to live, get in."

We decided to get in.

The back section of the van was empty, windowless, and painted the same shiny black as the outside. There were no seats and nothing to hold on to – nothing to do but squeeze in and crouch down on the floor.

Officer Reeve slammed the door closed as soon as we were all inside, plunging us into complete darkness. I felt the van dip slightly as he returned to the driver's seat. With the rumble of an engine, the van suddenly lurched forward and I was thrown sideways into Jordan.

"Sorry," I muttered.

But that first bump turned out to be the least of our worries. For the next ten minutes we were jolted around in every direction, struggling to avoid getting slammed up against the walls or each other as the van cut a path through the wasteland.

Finally, Officer Reeve pulled to a stop.

"Where do you reckon he's —"

But Peter's voice was drowned out by a sudden blast of noise from outside — an enormous mechanical clunking so loud that the whole van vibrated with the force of it. After a few seconds, the clunking gave way to a clattering of wheels and a low screech of metal against metal.

Something was moving out there. Something big. And then whatever it was pulled to a stop and the noise died away.

The van started driving again. About thirty seconds later, the screeching and clattering returned, more quietly this time, fading behind us as we drove off.

For a few minutes, the ride was as bumpy as ever, but then Reeve took a sharp left and the ground under us instantly became smooth and flat.

"Now what?" Jordan whispered. "What do we say when he lets us out?"

"Play dumb," said Peter desperately. "Just act like we don't know what –"

"He caught us *outside* the wall!" I hissed at him. "How are we supposed to play dumb about that?"

No answer. No one said anything else for the rest of the journey.

After maybe half an hour, the ground got rougher again – not nearly as bad as before, but enough for me to realize that we'd gone off the road. I'd barely had time to adjust to the change when the van rumbled to a stop and Officer Reeve opened the door to let us out.

The three of us staggered out of the van.

We were back in Phoenix. On the edge of it, anyway. Officer Reeve had driven around onto the grass at the eastern end of town, near the track that led out to the airport. I guess he didn't want to cause a scene by parading us through the town center.

"Come with me," he said, locking the door. "And don't try anything stupid or you'll wind up in even worse trouble."

I had a hard time imagining how that could be possible, but I didn't have the head space to come up with an escape plan. And even if we did get away from Officer Reeve, today had made it pretty clear that there was nowhere to run to.

Reeve led us towards the security center, and I vaguely registered that we were on the same street that Mr. Ketterley had guided Mum and me through on the day we'd first arrived. I didn't remember shaking quite so much the first time around.

A few people turned to look at us as we went past, but Officer Reeve just smiled and waved at them like there was nothing going on.

The path opened up onto the end of the main street and Reeve started walking faster. He had a look of pained indecision on his face, like he wanted to get us inside the security center as soon as possible, but wasn't sure what to do with us when we got there.

At the other end of the street, near the mall, I could still see plenty of people going for walks and finishing dinners. I thought about shouting out to them, but who were they going to believe – their friendly neighborhood security guard, or three no-good teenagers who'd been caught breaking curfew?

So I kept my mouth shut and followed Officer Reeve up the steps to the security center.

There was a shuffling sound behind me, and I glanced back to see Jordan with her hand down near the bushes. I raised an eyebrow at her, but she shook her head.

Reeve stopped at the top of the steps. "Do everything Calvin tells you," he said out of the corner of his mouth, "and keep your mouths shut unless you're spoken to."

He pushed open the door and waved the three of us inside.

Chapter 29

The little room we stepped into looked less like part of a police station and more like the waiting room of a really classy doctor's office. There were red padded chairs all around the outside, and the walls were hung with massive abstract oil paintings that looked like they were supposed to be of doves or something.

At the far end of the room, another man in a black security uniform was sitting behind a counter, scribbling something on a notepad. He looked up as the door opened, and sent Officer Reeve a questioning look.

"Get Calvin," said Reeve.

The guy nodded and slipped out into the hallway behind him.

A second later, Calvin limped into the room. He'd come without his crutch and he had to lean on the counter for support. His eyes flashed across each of our faces and his expression turned dangerous.

"I picked up these three on my way back into town," said Reeve.

Calvin straightened up against the counter. "*Where?*" he demanded.

"They were out on the main road, sir," said Reeve, stiffening slightly. "Just short of the road works. No bikes or anything."

I stared at Reeve. He was *covering* for us. I tried to keep my expression neutral, tried to act like this version of the story wasn't news to me.

"I see," said Calvin, leaning forward. "And you're sure they didn't –"

"I'm not sure of anything, sir. They said they'd gotten lost on a bushwalk."

Calvin studied us, clearly suspicious. Then he took a step away from the counter. "Thank you,

Reeve," he nodded. "This way, children."

He turned on his good leg and hobbled back into the hallway.

I shot Officer Reeve a backwards glance as we followed Calvin out of the room, but he refused to make eye contact. He turned away and began talking to the guy behind the counter.

At the other end of the hallway was a big open-plan office space, which I assumed would be full of security guards during the day, but was now almost deserted. The few people who were still there looked up curiously as we went past.

Calvin led us down another hallway and into the first place in this whole building that my brain could compare to the cop shows I'd seen on TV. An interrogation room.

A square table stood bolted to the floor in the middle of the room, with a metal folding chair facing it on either side. The panel lighting in the ceiling flickered on automatically, harsh and bright. I felt really exposed all of a sudden – which I guess was the idea.

"Sit," said Calvin. He pointed into the corner of the room where a couple of extra chairs were leaning against the wall.

Peter and I unfolded them and sat down next to Jordan.

Calvin lowered himself into the chair on the opposite side. "Explain yourselves," he demanded.

"What do you mean?" asked Peter earnestly. "We were bushwalking, like Officer Reeve said."

"Bushwalking. At seven o'clock at night?"

"No!" said Peter. "Well, okay, yeah, we were. But not on purpose! We started at lunchtime on one of the walking tracks."

"Ask Luke's mum!" Jordan added. "She saw us leave."

"We didn't mean to break the curfew, but we got lost," I said, corroborating Officer Reeve's story. "By the time we found our way out to –"

Calvin held up a hand and I closed my mouth.

"I was under the impression that those walking tracks were quite clearly marked," he said.

"I guess so." I shrugged feebly.

"And yet the three of you somehow wandered so far off course that you weren't able to find your way back to civilization until well after nightfall?"

"Y-yeah," I said, fully aware of how ridiculous it sounded.

"Lucky Officer Reeve came past and found us," said Peter, trying to deflect attention from my obvious lie.

"Very," said Calvin coldly. He wasn't buying it.

My mind flashed back to the conversation we'd heard in Crazy Bill's recording. Calvin had been ordered to keep the peace. *We can't afford a blood bath.* That's what the other guy had said to him. I tried to reassure myself that Calvin wasn't allowed to touch us, that he'd been ordered to keep things nonviolent.

But the look on Calvin's face told a different story. He definitely didn't *look* nonviolent.

"Tell me," he said, struggling to his feet again so that he was towering over the top of us, "did you come across anything interesting in your travels?"

"Not really," I said. A trickle of sweat snaked its way down my spine.

"We saw a kangaroo with one eye poked out," said Peter. He seemed to be coming back to life a bit. I guess he was back in familiar territory now, talking his way out of trouble. "He was doing okay, though. Hopping around in circles, but –"

Calvin's eyes narrowed. "That is not what I meant."

"Oh," said Peter innocently. "What did you mean, then?"

Calvin didn't answer. His eyes bored into us, willing us to crack and give something away.

But Peter had cornered him. If we *did* know something, Calvin was desperate to get it out of us. But if we *didn't*, the last thing he wanted to do was give anything away.

"Hand me your backpack," he ordered suddenly, stretching a hand across the table towards Jordan.

I shot her a panicked look. The book was still in there, and so was the copy of *Time* magazine that Jordan had snatched from the warehouse. As soon as Calvin opened the bag, he'd know exactly where we'd been and what we'd been doing. But what choice did Jordan have?

She shrugged the backpack off her shoulders and handed it over. Calvin upended the bag, spilling its contents out onto the table. An empty water bottle rolled off and clattered onto the floor.

I scanned the pile and immediately realized that something was up. No book. No magazine. How was that…

Jordan. She must have dropped them in the bushes on the way in. Good thing one of us was able to keep their head in a crisis.

"Hmph," said Calvin, clearly disappointed. Then, like he was scrambling for *something* to get us in trouble for, he picked up Jordan's pocket knife and said, "I'm going to have to confiscate this."

"Yes, sir," said Jordan meekly.

Calvin threw the empty bag back at her and she started gathering her stuff into it.

"You three seem to have an unfortunate knack for getting yourselves into trouble," he said. "I may need to have a word with your principal and see if we can find something more constructive for you to do with your time."

I barely had time to wonder what that could mean before a deafening *SMASH* suddenly exploded from the hallway behind us.

There were panicked shouts, then running footsteps, the sound of shattering glass, and an all-too-familiar barely human growling.

Crazy Bill was on the loose.

"Stay here," Calvin barked, jumping to his feet and hopping out of the room as fast as his one working leg could carry him. He slammed the door shut and started shouting at someone in the hallway. "WHERE IS HE?"

"Down the hall," said a breathless woman. "Ben's gone after him."

My stomach plummeted as I recognized the voice. It was Ms. Pryor.

"I thought you had him restrained to the –" she began.

"We did, but he got away, I don't know how –"

Calvin swore. He must have reached for his gun, because a second later Pryor shouted, "Put that down! We need him alive, Bruce! If this is a side effect of the fallout, then we need to –"

But another enormous crash – like something heavy being thrown against a wall – drowned out the rest of her words and the two of them thundered away down the hall.

We heard more shouting, further away this time, and more things getting chucked around and smashed. Crazy Bill was angry. And as usual, he wasn't holding back.

And then, suddenly, it all stopped. For ten minutes, we didn't hear anything else. Peter opened his mouth to say something, but Jordan told him to shut up. There was every chance that we were being recorded.

Some dark part of me started hoping that Crazy Bill had managed to finish Calvin off this time. Or, better yet, that they'd finished off each other. But I had a suspicion it wasn't going to be that simple.

We were almost at the point of going out there to see what was happening when we heard footsteps coming down the hall.

The door opened and Calvin hobbled back into

the room. He was red in the face and his normally tidy hair was pointing in all directions.

"Your parents are coming to get you," he said. He didn't look happy about it.

We followed him out of the interrogation room, and I immediately wondered why Calvin had needed to ask Ms. Pryor where Crazy Bill had gone. The path of destruction leading down the hallway seemed to make the answer to that question pretty clear.

As we went along, I had to step over a fallen door that lay broken on the ground. Not just torn off its hinges – this thing was snapped in half. A bit further up, there was a giant crack in one of the walls.

But it wasn't until we got back out into the big office area that we realized just how much damage Crazy Bill had done. The whole room was a mess of upturned tables and smashed computer monitors. Bits of plaster were still raining down from the ceiling. An air conditioning unit had somehow been torn from the roof and was now lying in a crumpled heap in the middle of the room.

Calvin led us back into the waiting room where

we'd first arrived. It was completely untouched –
obviously the struggle had ended out in the hall.

The front door swung open and Ms. Pryor strode
back into the building, holding a tissue up against her
bleeding nose.

"All under control?" said Calvin sharply.

Pryor nodded. "He's being transferred now."

"And Ben?"

"Nothing life-threatening."

"Good."

The guard behind the counter was sitting calmly
at his computer, doing a good job of pretending that
a superpowered maniac hadn't just trashed half the
building. Calvin muttered something to him in an
undertone, then he and Ms. Pryor disappeared down
the hall again without a backwards glance.

"Transferred?" Jordan whispered, sitting down in
one of the seats along the wall.

"Yeah," I said, "whatever that means."

I could see that Jordan wanted to keep
speculating, but I didn't have the energy for it. I
collapsed across three seats, closed my eyes, and

waited for Mum to arrive.

It had been the mother of all long days. And we were still alive at the end of it, which was more than I'd been expecting. But even that thought wasn't much comfort.

The end of the world was still looming.

And if the last eleven days were any clue, things were only going to get weirder from here on out.

Chapter 30

"So, let's review," said Peter, unscrewing the top of his Coke bottle. "We're trapped in the middle of nowhere by a wall and a wasteland and a bunch of men with guns. We've got Calvin and Pryor breathing down our necks, and even if we get around them, we've got no idea what to do next because they've just *transferred* our only source of information, and he was a homicidal nut case anyway. We can't call for help, and we can't tell anyone else what's going on because we'd be putting them in as much danger as us. Is that pretty much the size of it?"

"And there are eighty-eight days until the end of the world," I added.

"Right, that too."

It was Sunday afternoon and we were sitting out in the park eating fish and chips.

All of our parents had swallowed the story about us accidentally getting lost in the bush. I'd felt bad about lying to Mum, but I guess it was better than the alternative.

Jordan and Peter seemed to have left yesterday's argument behind. I guess they'd come to some unspoken agreement that their harsh words were a result of all the stress we'd been under.

I looked up and saw Cathryn coming past, probably on her way to the mall. Although I knew he'd seen her, Peter refused to even acknowledge her existence.

"You know what?" he said instead, reaching for the chips. "I'm glad I met you guys. Imagine all the fun I'd be missing out on if you hadn't –"

"Officer Reeve!" called Jordan suddenly, getting to her feet.

Reeve wasn't in uniform, so it took me a minute to spot him. He was walking across the playground, talking to a curly haired woman and carrying a little boy up on his shoulders – his wife and son, I assumed. He glanced up to see who had called his name, then pushed on towards the park as though he hadn't seen us.

Peter bundled up the fish and chips and the three of us went over to meet him.

"Hi," I said as we reached the playground.

Reeve shot me a frustrated look and then turned to his wife and sighed, "Won't be a sec."

He wrangled his son down from his shoulders with his one good arm, wincing a bit as the boy slid down his battered body. He set him loose on the playground, then pulled us aside.

"What's the matter?" I asked.

"We shouldn't be talking," said Reeve uncomfortably.

"We just wanted to thank you for last night," said Jordan. "For not –"

"Sure," Reeve cut her off. "No worries." He moved to walk away.

"What were you doing out there anyway?" said Peter.

Reeve stiffened. "Nothing. Just a patrol run."

"How did you bring us back inside?" I asked. "Is there a gate?"

"Stop!" hissed Reeve. "Don't even – look, I know you kids are trying to get to the bottom of everything that's going on out here. But I can't help you."

"So why did you cover for us last night, then?" snapped Jordan. "If you're not interested in helping –"

"Because if I'd told Calvin the truth, you'd all be dead by now."

Jordan opened her mouth, and then closed it again. She stared down at the grass.

Officer Reeve glanced back over his shoulder to where his wife was pushing their kid on a swing. It dawned on me that his story about winding up in Phoenix probably wasn't all that different from ours.

"Listen," he said, his eyes back on us. "You need to know that last night was a one-off. Next time you kids get yourselves into strife, I won't be able to bail you out. If it was just me, then maybe, but I won't put my family in harm's way."

"Yeah," said Jordan. "Yeah, you're right. I'm sorry."

"I don't know the half of what Shackleton and his mates are up to," Reeve said. "But I've seen enough to know that they're willing to do whatever it takes to make sure their secrets *stay* secret. You kids are better off keeping your heads down – you don't want to get tangled up in all of that."

"Right," I said, wishing it were that simple.

"Good on you," Officer Reeve smiled, clapping me on the shoulder.

He'd almost made it back to the playground when Peter called, "Hang on!"

Reeve wheeled around. "*What?*"

"Our bikes," said Peter. "We left them out by the side of the road, near the boom gate guarding that warehouse place. Could you...?"

Officer Reeve shot Peter a pained look. "All right," he sighed, like he was being talked into it against his better judgment. "Okay, yeah, I'll get them for you. But that's *it*. That's the last I want to hear from you three."

We all nodded fervently at him, then left the poor guy in peace and went back to our spot on the grass.

Peter sat against a tree and started tossing our leftover chips at an ibis that was walking past.

Meanwhile, Jordan flipped open a design and tech textbook from her bag and started highlighting important sentences. It took my brain a second to even process what she was doing. It didn't seem right that we still had homework to deal with on top of everything else.

Then again, we'd probably have to make an extra effort to get it all done from now on if we wanted to stay out of trouble with Ms. Pryor.

I lay back on the grass, wishing I could take Reeve's advice and forget that any of this had ever happened.

I wanted a way out. I wanted someone else to come in and take over. I wanted to wake up and find out that all of it was a dream.

I wanted *something* to happen so that I could go back to my old life where my dad was only a phone call away, and China had the monopoly on giant walls, and the only thing homeless people wanted from you was spare change.

But I knew that wasn't happening. Not unless

the three of us somehow found a way to put a stop to whatever the Shackleton Co-operative was planning. Three kids against an evil billionaire corporate empire.

The sun beat down on my face, and I closed my eyes. I'd only woken up a couple of hours ago, but I was still exhausted from the day before.

I guess it takes more than one sleep-in to make up for –

Suddenly, my eyes snapped open again.

A noise from somewhere across the park – barely audible, but definitely there. I couldn't place it at first. It'd been so long since…

I looked over at the others. They'd heard it too.

Jordan dropped her textbook on the grass. "Is that…?"

"Yeah," I said.

Someone's phone was ringing.

Chris Morphew
The PHOENIX FILES
RESTRICTED AREA 39
contact

mutation
The PHOENIX FILES
Chris Morphew

Chris Morphew
The PHOENIX FILES
underground

coming soon

Someone in Phoenix is plotting

to wipe out the human race.

And the clock is already ticking.

THERE ARE ONE HUNDRED DAYS

UNTIL THE END OF THE WORLD.

Born in Sydney, Australia, in 1985, Chris Morphew spent his childhood writing stories about dinosaurs and time machines. More recently he has written for the best-selling *Zac Power* series. *The Phoenix Files* is his first series for young adults.